Sarah Francis was born in and brought up in Yorkshire. She read English at Oxford University, since when she has been writing full time. Her first novel, *Odd Fish and Englishmen*, was published in 1996. *Angels in the Architecture* is her second novel. She lives in London with her husband and two daughters.

Also by Sarah Francis

ODD FISH AND ENGLISHMEN

Angels in the

Architecture

Sarah Francis

Dedication

For Aggie and Nou. And for B.

An *Abacus* Book

First published in Great Britain by Abacus in 1999
This edition published by Abacus in 2000

A CIP catalogue record for this book
is available from the British Library.

ISBN 0 349 11232 0

Typeset in Perpetua by M Rules
Printed and bound in Great Britain by
Clays Ltd, St Ives plc

Abacus
A Division of
Little, Brown and Company (UK)
Brettenham House
Lancaster Place
London WC2E 7EN

Chapter One

They buried him at midnight, beneath a fat midsummer moon, two lone figures and a bin bag. He had wanted to be laid beside the lighthouse, always a favourite haunt, but local outrage had made this impossible, so they rowed him out to sea and sank him in its reflection instead. Primrose hoped he would not mind – as his wife she had failed him too many times already – but when the final splash came, a bag of flour tied to either leg, his typewriter about his neck, it was too late to care anyway. With Johnny Macgregor reading from the ships log, the only book he had to hand, and Primrose attempting a few bars of Mozart's *Requiem* on her four-stringed guitar, Herb was gone, swallowed up by the sea he had spent his life crossing over. Only the clack-clack of their oars as they pulled themselves back to shore, and the dip-dip of the waves which led them there, gave any ceremony to what had been, but by then the rowers were tired and barely noticed. Stumbling back up the beach, Primrose to her bed on the roof, Johnny Macgregor to his on the sofa, they heard only the squawk of the returning wild turkeys, nothing more. Life went on.

Some said Herb died of a broken heart, others from more modern diseases, but according to Primrose it was just another of his whims. Indeed, had it not been for the intervention of Johnny Macgregor she might have left him just where she found him, crumpled beneath the steps, fists clenched at his chest, hating as she did to interfere in Herb's private affairs; but when it became clear this was one time he would not remonstrate, she made an exception and fetched a chair. Propping him upright on the deck, she made soup and talked about the weather, and when the sun grew hot she fetched him a hat and carried on. It did not matter that he could not answer her; if anything, this made it easier. After so many years, he owed her this one last chance at reconciliation, and without his arguments, she got it. Even Johnny Macgregor overcame his nervousness and came to sit at Herb's feet, not entirely comfortable with the situation, but grateful for the fact that he did not kick, and as afternoon faded into night, they made a reassuring family picture there, prone on the deck, finally at peace.

Their vigil lasted two days and seven hours, broken only by the fact that the wind had changed and they at last had to accept that Herb was past his best. Sliding him off the deck and down the beach, they were oblivious to the small crowd of horrified locals who had gathered to watch, and it was only when Johnny Macgregor was set upon while attempting to dig a hole in front of the souvenir shop, the closest he could get to the beloved lighthouse, that the need to negotiate Herb's end became clear. Ultimately convinced by the three-deep crowd of dissenters that this was not the place for Herb to rest, they dragged him back the way they had come and scooped him into the boat instead. And the rest is history. Only a single, slight figure standing on the cliffs above, observing yet unobserved, went without record, no one of a mind to recognise faces at this hour of night. But long after they had gone she remained there, her goodbyes for now her own, and as the sea took the two bags of flour, the typewriter, bin bag and body, and made of them what it would, she alone felt the loss. With the dawn she was gone, disappearing on the first ferry with the commuters and their tapping laptops, yet something in the air, in the patterns in the sand, would whisper she had been.

'Agatha came last night,' Primrose declared the next morning, hands on her hips, nose raised to the early sun. 'She was here, you know.'

And Johnny Macgregor, who had heard this theory too many times before and never known it to have substance, merely shrugged.

'She must have known he'd gone,' she continued, gesturing

out to sea and thus finding one more metaphor for the husband she had never liked to place.

'Maybe,' nodded Macgregor, although he thought no such thing.

'Definitely,' concluded Primrose, smiling and turning to face the man who was now her only friend. 'I always knew she'd be back.'

And with that Primrose was off, back up to the roof to disperse the last of the wild turkeys, satisfied that her job was done and she could get back to what she did so well: imagining what might have been, and wondering where it had all gone.

Chapter Two

When Primrose first met Herb on the 3.50 into Waterloo, looking up from her Mills & Boon to find him sitting next to her, she decided almost immediately that this was the man she had been waiting for. Something to do with the fact that he ignored her, so intent upon writing that even when she half sat upon his knee when the train jolted at Clapham Junction, his only response was a quick tug to his raincoat and a flick of the page. Within minutes she was planning introductions, mentally dropping handkerchiefs as she sorted through her pick-up lines, but when they pulled into Waterloo and he jumped out before she had even got to her feet, it was clear such seductions would be a challenge. Following him down the platform, she had to run just to keep him in sight, and when he jumped on to

a bus headed for the West End, she almost killed herself dodging traffic to reach the next stop before it did. Heaving and
panting in exhaustion, she dropped into a seat just behind him
and wondered exactly what she was doing. But when she saw
he was writing again, head bent, pencil jumping with every
pot-hole in the road, she knew it made sense.

She watched him as far as Trafalgar Square, jumping off in
the same flurry of scavenging pigeons, striding behind him up
the Charing Cross Road, but when he disappeared through the
stage door of Wyndham's Theatre even she lacked the ingenuity
to tackle the stage doorman, and she had to let him go. So she
wandered around to the box office, buying a ticket for that
evening's performance without even seeing what it was, and
she took her place in the stalls, furiously turning the programme
inside out in an attempt to find his face; it was the interval
before she spotted him standing in the wings. When the curtain
swung down and the audience filed out for their gin and tonics,
she sat there transfixed, wondering if this was the love she had
read about for so long. If this was the searing, not-to-be-
thwarted passion that too many years imagining herself a heroine
had insisted she was born for. She could only cross her legs and
hope.

Ten minutes before the end of the play – a murder-
mystery by Agatha Christie; she never did find out
whodunnit – she squeezed out of her seat and left the theatre
to wait outside the stage door. When he appeared half an hour
or so later, linking arms with a couple of the actors, she tried

to catch his eye as they moved towards the street, but a crowd of girls with autograph books were too quick for her, and by the time Primrose got close, the circle around them was tight and ungiving. And so she waited, leaning against one of the review boards that flanked the theatre, and when at last they were finished, the three men sighing and nudging one another towards Compton's in Soho, she was behind them, waiting for her chance. When the rest of the cast joined them minutes later, forming a knot at the bar which she did not dare untangle, she told herself there was no hurry, and concluded that introductions could wait.

She followed Herb for over three weeks, seeking him out on the 3.50 every afternoon, shadowing him until he boarded the 11.27 back again each night. She knew where he lived, which newspaper he read, how he wore red socks on Mondays but blue the rest of the week, and that he preferred to drink coffee although tea would invariably do. She even came to predict those days he would be writing and those when he would do nothing more than stare at the window, looking through her reflection at the blurring landscape. And because she knew these things, she believed she knew him.

And then one day, while she was waiting in the café opposite Wyndham's for the play to end, he burst out of the stage door a good half an hour before the interval and charged away down the street. Throwing coins at the café owner, for whom she had represented his best business in years, she ran out after him, catching him as he crossed the road in front of the

National Portrait Gallery, and for the first time since Clapham Junction almost a month ago, reaching out to touch him, asking him to wait.

He spun around, a broad smile suffusing his face, but when he saw it was her, a stranger and not the person he had been expecting, he seemed confused. 'Yes?' he asked, detaching his arm from her hand.

Primrose hesitated. 'You're early,' she told him. 'Are you all right?'

'What?'

'You're early. Why have you left in the middle of the performance? What about Poirot's cummerbund?' After watching the performance a dozen times, she knew the intricacies of his job as a dresser down to the last sock and shoe. (It was the stage doorman who had given his job away; the rest she had figured out for herself.) 'He can never tie it properly on his own.'

Herb stared at her, glancing from her yellow velvet mini-dress to her purple tights. 'Are you mad?'

She shook her head. 'Sorry,' she offered. 'I know it must sound bizarre, but I've been following you.' He jerked backwards from her, but she caught his arm and tried again. 'Not following, exactly, just watching.' Rephrasing it seemed to offer little consolation.

'You're obviously completely out of your mind.' He looked at her, then at his arm where she held it.

'I'm not, I promise,' Primrose pleaded. 'I'm sorry. It's just . . .' She paused, dropping her head as the words refused to come. 'It's just I was worried about you. I've kind of got used to your routine, and, well, you never leave before the end of the show. I thought something might be wrong. I'm sorry.' She sighed hopelessly, suddenly aware of how ridiculous she sounded, and released her grip on his arm.

But Herb did not move. Staring at her, he watched a tear well and then slip from her downcast eyes, and softened. 'No, no, I'm sorry,' he told her. He stepped towards her, and took her arm. 'I'm just feeling a bit . . .' He left the sentence hanging in the air, then snatched it back again. 'A bit in need of a drink,' he finished, overly cheery but good enough for Primrose. 'Come on, stranger, I'll buy you a beer.'

They went to a pub just behind St Martin-in-the-Fields, taking a table in the corner and both ordering halves. Primrose was quiet now, rather overwhelmed at having caught what she had chased, and as Herb went back to the bar for some smoky bacon crisps, she could only sit and stare at her hands.

'Are you all right?' He was beside her again, handing her a paper bag with a pig on the front.

She shook her head. 'I don't eat meat.'

'Me neither,' he admitted. 'Just these things.' He offered her one, and she took it. 'It's all fake,' he insisted. 'No piggies in here.'

Primrose put it in her mouth and tried to chew. But as she did, the tears that had started outside began to flow properly, and despite Herb quickly snatching the packet back, claiming it was a bit of fun, that was all, she only sobbed louder.

Ducking his head to avoid the curious stares now coming from the bar, Herb shushed her as comfortingly as his embarrassment would allow him, handing her a beer mat to blot her face, then marvelling when she used it. Slowly, noisily, she began to calm down.

She wiped her face, and looked up at him with soggy, fading eyes, her cheeks flush with dye from the beer mat. 'I'm such an idiot,' she told him. He shrugged, not in a position to argue. 'I'm so sorry. I'm just a bit overwhelmed.' She took a deep breath, once, twice, and smoothed her hair back into its immaculately organised plaits. 'I'm Primrose,' she told him, offering her hand.

'Herb,' said Herb, taking it.

'I know,' said Primrose. She smiled gently, vaguely self-conscious. 'I've seen you about,' she explained, for he needed to hear something. 'On the train. At the theatre.'

Herb raised a finger, seeming to place her for a moment, then frowning. 'I thought I recognised you. It's from the train, is it?'

Primrose nodded. He didn't need to know about the rest, or not right now. 'So did you get fired?' she asked. This seemed the most obvious explanation.

He nodded. 'You know?'

'A guess. What happened.'

He shrugged. 'Nothing much. I wrote some letters, harmless notes really, but Brian, who plays Poirot, he took them a little seriously. And he made a complaint.' Herb shrugged again.

Primrose sighed exaggeratedly. 'You're a writer,' she told him, an assumption on her part but one he was happy to leave her with. 'Of course you would do that.' She pulled a strip from the sodden beer mat, and flicked it into the ashtray. 'And presumably he couldn't take the criticism. Didn't like someone more observant than himself picking him up on things. Well, whose loss is that?'

Herb shrugged. Apart from his obvious gain within the bounds of Primrose's imagination, he would have to say it was his. His loss. 'Mine,' he told her.

She rolled her eyes. 'His,' she insisted. 'His loss.' She mentally flicked through her programme, trying to put a face to her target. 'And they didn't give you a chance to explain? To defend yourself?'

Herb shook his head. How could he defend a year-long crush on a man it turned out had only been nice to him because he liked his costume well ironed? How could he defend his almost daily dispatches to someone he had followed from the Abbey in Dublin and done his utmost to take home with him ever since? How could he defend getting it so wrong? He shook his head. 'And say what?'

'But it's so unfair.'

'Yes,' murmured Herb, although not for the same reasons.

Primrose gazed at him, thinking him heroic. 'You are incredible.'

'Thank you.' He felt slightly fraudulent, but because this was nothing new, he chose to ignore it. 'And you're very kind.'

Primrose smiled, accepting the compliment and intending to improve upon it. 'Have you eaten tonight?' She knew he usually got a snack on Old Compton Street on his way home, but obviously there would be none of that tonight. As expected, he shook his head. 'Then come on,' she told him, pushing both their empty glasses to the other side of the table. 'I'm buying us dinner to commiserate.'

She stood up, pulling him after her, and as he reached for his coat and wondered what he was letting himself in for, she handed him the untouched bag of crisps with a smile.

'Sorry about that, it was just a joke,' he apologised.

'Don't worry about it. It was funny. Really it was.'

They took the bus to Hampstead where her parents lived, getting off at the Royal Free Hospital and walking up the hill to a restaurant called Keats, a reference she thought he would enjoy given his obvious literariness. Thick green curtains covered the windows, and as they were led to their table at the back of the second room, Herb eyed up the other diners and felt disastrously out of place.

'Isn't this a bit smart?' he hissed.

Primrose waved her hand dismissively. 'Don't worry,' she told him. 'They know my parents really well. We always turn up in whatever.'

Herb nodded, taking the menu, then putting it back again. 'You choose. You know what's best.' He sat back, feeling in his pockets for his cigarettes. 'Can I smoke?' he asked.

Primrose answered by taking one for herself, lighting it on the candle in the centre of their table and dragging heavily.

Herb smiled approvingly. 'Your parents . . .?' He looked around, as if expecting them to be at the next table.

Primrose tilted her head towards the street. 'Italy,' she told him, 'Tuscany, poking around churches and things. I'm on my own.'

'On your own? You live at home?'

Primrose nodded. 'Just over the road, opposite the church.' She seemed vaguely apologetic. 'I haven't got around to moving out yet.'

Herb pulled a face. 'They're not short of a quid or two, then?' He was waving at the restaurant, but meant Hampstead.

'No. I suppose not. I've never really thought about it.'

'There's your answer.'

Primrose considered her cutlery and waited for him to continue. He was silent. 'Does it bother you?' she asked, remembering how she had offered to pay for dinner. She would hate to steal his thunder at this early stage.

He shook his head. 'It's only money.'

Primrose grinned. That had always been her attitude too.

Primrose called the waiter across and ordered Herb a steak, medium-well, and a salad for herself. 'So what will you do now?' she asked. 'Now you're not working and everything.'

Herb ran a cocktail stick beneath his fingernails, then sat back decisively. 'Actually, I've been thinking of getting away, going somewhere completely new.' He began buttering a roll.

'A fresh start and all that.' It would be some time before the scandal of the letters, found by the stage manager and read aloud during Notes, died down and saw him working in the West End again.

Primrose nodded.

'There's always America. My mother was American, so I have the passport.' He fumbled in his pocket and held it up to show her.

'You carry it with you?'

'Everywhere. You never know.'

Primrose nodded, flicking through to look at his picture, then handing it back. He continued, 'I've got a cousin in New York. Maybe I'll get myself work on Broadway.'

'Or we could just take a bus and travel, look for America, like in the song.' She started humming Simon and Garfunkel's 'America', her favourite song of '68. Herb pulled a face, more at the 'we' of the thing than the reference. She ignored him. 'I've even got a visa for it already, would you believe?'

Herb shook his head. He wouldn't.

Primrose nodded triumphantly. 'Summer holiday,' she told him. 'My passport came back from the Embassy only last week. It must be a sign.'

'What was that song you said?' Herb asked, hoping to change the subject to something less ominous.

'You don't know it? Hang on.'

She stood up and walked across the restaurant to the bar at the other side. Tilting back in his chair to watch her, he saw her gesture towards the record player on the far side of the counter, then lean across to sort through the covers stacked in front of it. Herb returned to his wine, filling up his glass from the bottle and settling back.

'Or there's Australia,' he considered, as Primrose slipped back into her chair beside him. 'I have family there too.'

Primrose held her finger to her lips and nodded to the speaker just above their table. 'Listen,' she mouthed.

He listened. It was all about lovers and married fortunes and strangely placed real estate kept in a bag. He shook his head and glanced at Primrose. 'And?' he asked.

Primrose smiled tentatively, her eyes glittering as she slunk forwards across the table. 'The song's about us, Herb, can't you hear?'

He listened again, catching something about cigarettes, and lighting one in agreement. 'Weird, huh?' he mumbled.

Primrose shook her head, her heart racing as she had read it was supposed to. And while Paul Simon sang of spies and gabardine coats, she took Herb's face in her hands and kissed him. 'No, Herb,' she breathed, her left plait tracing spider's legs across his buttered roll. 'No, Herb,' she told him, 'it's Fate.'

Fate was a beloved word in Herb's dictionary, slipped between 'fat' and 'father', the two things in the world he was most afraid of, and providing just the excuse his life needed. Indeed, it had been Fate that had initially got him into the theatre, a chance meeting with the Abbey wardrobe assistant in a pub in

Donegal giving new hope to the boy with the spare tyres whom everyone expected to take over the family farm. And it had been Fate that brought him to London, a brief flirtation with an actor who would later get him fired, introducing Herb to a part of his character he had not known existed but would nevertheless diet for years to fit into. And now, it seemed, it was Fate that had brought him Primrose, just when his luck was down and there seemed nowhere to go, and as the song ended but Primrose kept singing, he wondered where it would take him this time.

Herb agreed to go with Primrose because she asked. Had she offered him a cup of tea and a garibaldi, he would have given her exactly the same response. Nothing to do with the song she was humming or the two bottles of wine they had drunk, and not really anything to do with Primrose herself, other than the fact that she promised to love him indefinitely and follow wherever he went. With a habit of seizing opportunities, and a need to get as far away from men called Brian as was physically – and legally – possible, quite simply, it was an offer he could not refuse. And so, just as would any out-of-work, self-respecting dresser, he stuck a pin in her cheque-book, a curtain ring from the green velvet drapes on her finger, and decided East Coast America was the place to be.

'My parents get back on Monday,' Primrose told him. 'I just have to be around until then. To feed the cat. And tell them.'

Herb frowned, unimpressed by such trivialities.

'It's just a few days,' she cajoled. 'We can stay at the house.'

Herb shrugged, silent as she paid the bill, then followed sullenly as she led him from the restaurant and down the street the four or five hundred yards to her parents' house, a rather faded-looking Georgian house set back from the road. 'If I'm going, I want to go now,' he murmured as she turned her key in the lock and waved him inside. He gazed around at the dimly lit hallway and the carpeted wooden staircase leading upstairs. 'Now or never.' Time had taught him that even Fate could stand a little bullying.

Primrose closed the door behind her and leaned back against it, chewing her plait and staring at him intently. 'Now?' she asked. 'This minute?'

'Well, tomorrow,' he accommodated. He did not want to be unreasonable.

'And not tell my parents? Or feed the cat? Or find somewhere where we can stay when we get there?'

Herb shrugged, moving across to the hall table where a tower of cheap paperbacks offered their own conclusion upon the matter. He sighed, fingering the top copy. 'Your choice,' he told her.

Primrose wavered.

And because Primrose had spent her life trying to avoid making decisions, and believed being with someone to be the means of keeping on doing this, she opted for the latter and picked up her coat. 'I just have to open some tins for the cat,' she told him, 'and pick up some bits and pieces.'

She scooted downstairs to the kitchen, scribbling a hurried note to her parents about airplanes and savings accounts and how they needed to buy Whiskas, then returned to the hall. 'I'm ready,' she announced, just as Herb was beginning to think he wasn't. 'Let's go.'

And they went, Herb carrying Primrose's vanity case full of the knick-knacks she couldn't bring herself to leave behind, Primrose swinging empty arms. They did not speak all the way up the street and into the taxi, an awareness of how much there was to say making silence preferable, and as they reached Heathrow, pulling up in front of Departures and unloading their single bag, it was the lack of conversation that kept them going. When the woman at the BOAC desk began to confirm the details of the two tickets for New York the next day, Primrose waved her cheque-book dismissively and told her not to bother. And when they handed the man at passports their boarding cards and he asked them the nature of their trip, their response was much the same, for they knew what they were doing, thank you very much, and didn't need to explain themselves to him.

They spent their first night together – such as it was – in the Departures lounge, Herb flicking through a stack of Agatha Christies he had bought in Duty Free, Primrose writing postcards.

'Will you write on the plane?' she asked, her own scribbling reminding her of the many journeys spent watching him fill his notebook.

'I'll probably phone,' he told her, assuming she was referring to the cousin he had already suggested they might stay with. 'There's no point wasting money on hotel rooms while we wait for them to get a letter.'

Primrose nodded politely. 'Actually, I meant "write" write,' she revealed, leaning on the word to emphasise its greater importance. 'Isn't that what you do?'

'Write?' asked Herb.

Primrose nodded, watching him close his copy of *Murder on the Nile*, and consider for a moment. 'I thought you were a writer,' she began, ready to apologise for the mistake. 'Sorry, I just assumed . . .'

'Well, I am, kind of,' Herb decided, for if his letters were to achieve anything, it should at least be that. 'I don't do it seriously,' he told her, much as he had insisted to the stage manager. 'It's just a hobby, really. Something I like to do.'

Primrose gazed at her postcards and smiled. 'I always wanted to marry a writer.' She did not mention that she would just as happily have settled for an architect or doctor instead, and chose to ignore the look of horror that flashed across Herb's face at the mention of marriage. She thought for a moment, then asked, 'Novels?'

Herb nodded. Why not?

'Better still,' Primrose murmured. And while Herb wondered how it had come to this, Primrose twiddled her stolen curtain ring and marvelled at the ease with which she had become a wife.

Chapter Three

As he had planned, Herb called his cousin as soon as they landed at JFK, reaching him at home and quickly accepting his offer to pick them up. When Dan, a deputy in the New York Police Department, arrived, parking his squad car on double yellows just outside the doors and striding inside to find them, they were perched either end of a row of orange plastic seats like two bookends, fading beneath the fluorescent lighting of the airport. In the lateness of another time zone, Primrose's enthusiasm for the fairy-tale she had envisaged was wobbling slightly, and with her dress stained red from an accident with some tomato juice and her tights now sagging haplessly about her knees, she was beginning to question quite how happy-ever-after this was turning out to be. But when Herb introduced her to his cousin as his new best friend, and held the door open when she climbed into the back of the squad car, she cheered up a little, and slid into the car with renewed vigour.

As they skimmed over the Hudson Bridge towards Manhattan, Herb and Dan up front, Primrose dozing on the back seat, the lights of the city glittered in the distance, and the mood was easy. Catching up on family news, who had shamed or married whom, which in-law had been outlawed, Dan made approving gestures towards the sleeping Primrose and told him he had done well.

'We had our worries about you for a while there,' he grinned, 'when we heard you were working in the theatre.' He winked playfully and thrust his elbow into Herb's arm.

Herb flinched and rubbed at his sleeve. 'Meaning?' he asked defensively. Then, less sternly, 'you're one to talk.' And he picked up Dan's police cap, dropping it on to his head and tilting it across one eye.

Dan threw it across the car, just missing the three or four inches of open window, and scowled. 'Don't kid around,' he warned. His eyes fixed on the road, he gestured for Herb to pick his cap up from the floor.

'So where you living now?' Unperturbed, Herb bent to pick it up, then tried it on himself, glancing in the mirror towards Primrose, and seeing she was asleep.

'Lower West Side,' Dan told him. 'Hell's Kitchen.' He shrugged. 'Course, Clare hates it, but that's normal. She wouldn't be Clare if she weren't bitching.'

Herb took off the cap and smoothed his hair. For the next five minutes they sat in silence, until left at a set of lights, then left again, they pulled up outside a large tenement building where Dan double-parked and reached back to swing open Primrose's door. She started awake, the lights of the city and the gentle banter of their conversation having lulled her, and she began to climb out, pulling her vanity case after her.

Dan turned towards Herb. 'I'm going to get Chinese food. You want to come?'

Herb looked at Primrose, now peering back inside the car, and then nodded. 'You don't mind, do you?' he checked.

Primrose looked worried.

'Fifth floor, first on the left,' Dan gestured.

She stepped back from the car, intending to move around to Herb's window, but as she did so, Dan caught the door with his finger and began to pull away. When she raised her hand and jumped forward, he stopped, grudgingly, winding down his window a crack and raising an eyebrow. But because Primrose only murmured something about saying goodbye, he simply grinned nonchalantly, wound it up again, and was gone. Somewhere in the retreating darkness, Herb thought he saw her wave, but by that time they were at the lights and he was more interested in Dan's suggestion that they use the siren.

'It is so good to see you, fella,' Herb exclaimed, as the car flashed blue and they headed towards Brooklyn. 'I haven't had this much fun in years.'

'And you won't,' promised Dan, always one to show family a good time. 'This is where it's at, kiddo. And don't let anyone,' he gestured backwards, indicating Primrose, 'tell you different.'

Alone on the street, watching the disappearing car flicker blue, then turn a corner, Primrose stared up at the building, its many windows cat's-eyed in the dark, curtained night. 'Fifth floor, first on the left,' she repeated to herself, and she pushed open the door and began climbing, too nervous to use the gated lift.

The fifth floor was the top, and by the time she got there she was heaving for breath and her tights had abandoned her to become spools of purple thread around her ankles.

'Clare, Clare, Clare,' she murmured to herself, as she climbed the last few steps and knocked on the door. Clare singular opened it.

'Hello, I'm Primrose.' She held out her hand.

'Hiya, Primrose.' Wearing a nightdress covered with a faded grey sweatshirt, Clare held wide the door and waved her inside, slamming it hard behind her and moving back towards the one piece of furniture the room possessed, a sofa. 'How ya doing?'

'Fine.' Primrose nodded uncomfortably, waiting to be invited to sit down, but no such offer coming. Remaining where she was, she gently placed her vanity case beside the door, and folded her hands.

'You alone then?' Clare asked, picking up a magazine and

flicking through it aggressively. Primrose watched her, the whole room echoing to the noise of slapped pages.

Primrose nodded. 'They've gone to pick up something to eat,' she apologised, reaching to pull up her tights but realising they were beyond such redemptions.

'Chinese food, yeah?' Clare frowned, still slamming paper. Primrose nodded. 'And you just let them go?'

Primrose shrugged. 'I was hungry too,' she told her. 'I thought it was all arranged.'

'Oh, it was arranged all right.' At last she closed the magazine, throwing it against the wall and turning to face Primrose. 'I warned him, the sonofabitch.' She shook her head resentfully. 'Poker.'

'Poker?' Primrose repeated. There was a moment of silence. 'Not Chinese food,' she confirmed.

'Poker,' Clare told her a second time. 'Those mean bastards have gone off to play poker, so Danny Boy can do what he always does with guests crazy enough to bunk with us and fleece them of every cent.'

Primrose moved away from the door and walked the two or three strides to the sofa, gazing around at the dark, peeling walls and linoed floor, and frowning disappointedly. 'So they're not coming back with something to eat?'

Clare shook her head. 'Not tonight they won't be. And God help them when they do.'

Primrose sat down next to her on the embattled sofa, all sunken and unsprung, and folded her arms. 'Well, this is fun,' she murmured. She thought for a moment, then looked up. 'Shall we go get something to eat ourselves then?'

Clare frowned. 'With what?' she demanded. 'I haven't even got the rent from three months ago, 'cause he lost it in a game.' She dropped her head on to the back of the sofa and groaned loudly. 'God, do I know how to pick them!'

Primrose stood up, patting Clare's knee. 'My shout.' She nudged her slumping body and grinned. 'Come on, we might as well.'

With a shrug, Clare stood up, swaying momentarily, then reached towards the radiator for her jeans and pulled them on over her nightdress and sweatshirt. 'You sure about this?' she asked quietly.

Primrose nodded.

Clare rubbed her forehead, thinking for a moment. 'D'ya like Vietnamese?' she asked, brightening. 'I'm supporting the cause and there's a great place under the bridge down by the freeway. I can't go there with Dan 'cause it's not strictly legal, but hey, you know what, fuck him!'

Primrose giggled, and nodded enthusiastically. She followed Clare towards the door, then she hesitated. 'It won't cause problems, our going, between the two of you?'

'Nah!' Clare shrugged. 'We got too many already.'

They took a cab to a tiny building tucked beneath a roaring bridge in a place Clare directed as Queens, and waited some four or five minutes outside a grey, splintering door before a small woman dressed in an apron let them in. Clare

shook her hand warmly, and they followed her down a corri-
dor and into a back room, where another ten or twelve people
sat in deep conversation around a large rectangular table.
Nodding to a couple of them, Clare sat down and beckoned
Primrose to join her.

'The great thing about this place is there's no menu,' she
told her. 'They just bring you what's good that day, or what they
feel like cooking. And it beats the pretzels and warm beer those
bastards will be getting.' She flicked back her head as she referred
to Dan and Herb, then frowned. 'You're not worried he's going
to lose every cent?' she asked. 'I can't believe you're so calm.'

Primrose shrugged. 'I suppose I feel lucky,' she smiled,
neglecting to mention that if Herb had a ten pound note in his
pocket it was only because she had lent it to him at the airport.

'Get you. I felt like that once. Now look at me.'

They sat back and poured eggcups of tea from the pot
which had been dropped on to their table. 'Cheers,' Clare
offered. 'Here's to you still feeling lucky tomorrow.'

Primrose smiled. 'Here's to us both.'

For the next hour or so Clare chipped and complained,
her terseness of mood partly circumstantial, partly character,
but when the tea was swapped for beer she let the last snipes of
irritation go, and finally began to relax. Pointing out various
other diners, she warmed to the occasion, and when at last
they staggered out to hail a cab, she had forgotten about her
plans to kill her husband, and was telling stories of when they
had first met.

'We went to Ireland for our honeymoon, which is where I met your Herb.' She grinned, leaning closer towards Primrose and giggling, her nightdress having escaped her jeans and hanging around her knees. 'I have to tell you, I was convinced he was queer,' she whispered, flapping her hand at the wrist. 'Guess I was wrong about that though, wasn't I?' She snorted as Primrose, in a haze of beer and jet lag, did her best to nod.

'Not Herb,' she murmured, pointing out a cab as it whizzed past on the bridge above their heads, and with the lights of the city twinkling across her face she took Clare's arm and grinned. 'Not Herb, he's mine.'

Not that night, he wasn't, for when they returned home half an hour later to discover the apartment just as they had left it, and the men still not back, Clare pointed Primrose towards the only bedroom and demanded she choose a side.

'They can make do with the couch,' she told her. 'If they ever bother to come home.' And she dropped on to the bed, clicking off the lamp in a single movement, and sighing loudly. Primrose struggled for a few minutes to stay awake, imagining that waiting for Herb would somehow bring him home sooner, but when her eyes began to close and the theory lost its attraction, she let her mind drift and within seconds was away.

When Dan and Herb got back the lights were out and the

apartment was quiet. Feeling for the bedroom door, Dan pointed Herb in the direction of the couch, then when he saw his bed taken, pointed himself there too. Groaning, he threw a couple of cushions on the floor and lay down, handing Herb a blanket and telling him to close the window if he got cold. 'I can't believe your luck,' he told him, for perhaps the twentieth time that night. Herb shrugged cleverly, and as the room slowly faded into life, he lay awake on the cushionless sofa, and hoped both fortune and springs would hold.

What seemed like minutes later, Clare was clattering around the kitchen making coffee, hoiking open the curtains with as much venom as she could instil to this simple task, and kicking at bodies. Raising his head, Dan rolled over and went back to sleep, but Herb, long awake, sat up, looked about for Primrose, then offered his hand.

'We met before,' Clare told him, ignoring the gesture and returning to the stove. 'How do you like it?' She held up the coffee pot. 'It only comes black.'

'Black then.' He rubbed at his eyes. 'Two sugars.'

'No sugar. We're sweet enough in this apartment. You'll have to make do as it is.'

Primrose appeared in the bedroom doorway, still in her runkled tights, although her dress had been exchanged for a housecoat of Clare's. 'Hello.'

'Hello.' Standing up, Herb held out his hand and Primrose walked towards him. She kissed his cheek, then pushed him down on the arm of the sofa.

'Aren't you wondering if we starved to death last night?' she asked him.

Herb shrugged, grinning. 'Aren't you wondering about what we did?'

Over at the stove, Clare coughed loudly, and banged a cupboard. 'Aren't you wondering how stupid we are?'

Flashing her yet another grin, Herb delved into his sleep-creased jean pocket, and pulled out a wad of papers. 'We played poker,' he announced, looking for a round of applause but meeting silence. He waited a moment. Nothing. 'And I won.'

'Won what?' Another cupboard slammed as Clare counted how many times she had heard this before. 'Chinese food?'

Herb shook his head, looking at Primrose and holding up the papers. 'I won a house,' he told them, laughing at the look of incredulity that had suffused their faces. 'I took a gamble, I got lucky, and I won a house.'

The house in question was an abandoned beach house some-where off Cape Cod, put up as a bail bond by a woman some four or five years ago, then left kicking around the police files after she disappeared. The officer who had lost it to Herb had himself won it only weeks earlier, a department tidy-up seeing many such assets find their way on to the poker table, and when he put it up against Herb and his marker of $550, he was happy to see it go. 'Good luck to you,' he had told Herb, as he

watched him dance from the table, papers fanning in all directions. 'You could have matched it with half the amount.' And
while Herb calculated exchange rates on his fingers, and Dan
did his best to organise a game for the next night in which they
could lose it again, the next shift arrived to hand over and the
night officers called it a day. Which brought them back to
now: Herb on the sofa arm, Dan on the floor, Clare slamming
cupboards, and Primrose squealing about real estate in pockets
and wondering where the song would end.

And they were back to the Fate thing again. When Dan woke
up and declared they would turn it into dollars before the
night was out, and Herb agreed, reminding her of all those
buses she had wanted to catch, Primrose held tight to the
papers and told him this was it. When Clare asked the
inevitable question of where he would have found the marker
he put up, and Dan offered thoughts on wives who supported
their men, Primrose continued to hug her deeds and stood
firm. In the time it took Herb to fetch a bag of sugar for the
now cold coffee, she ironed her old dress, gave back Clare's
housecoat, retrieved the untouched vanity case from beside the
door, and found America in an old diary of Dan's, quickly
locating the general area they were heading for and insisting
they get on. With the exact same single-mindedness that had
set her following Herb in the first place, she pointed to the
map, declared the fingernail of green their home, and had
them out the door and heading for the station without another

word. The deeds to the house safe in her case, only Herb apologising distracted her from her mission. But when she promised him she didn't mind, that she would have given him the money for the marker without a question, even he was quiet.

'You sure this is what you want?' he mumbled, fidgeting as they joined the queue for tickets.

'It's what I've always wanted,' she told him. And how could he argue with that?

Chapter Four

They caught a train north towards Providence and then on to
Boston, all the while glancing from the window to each other
just to make sure they were on the right track. Hurtling
down the wide flat plains of Massachussetts, Primrose was
reminded for a moment of the first time they had met, just a
few weeks ago, side by side on the clattering train, and she
leaned over to kiss his brow, to mark the moment. Herb
smiled, and squeezed her hand where it lay clenched beside
him on the seat. 'Happy?' he asked her, this habit of deciding
upon his own emotions by first asking about hers one that
would stick.

'Oh, yes,' breathed Primrose, without a second thought.

'Good,' nodded Herb, and he flicked his eyes towards her and away again. 'Me too.'

At the Boston Greyhound Terminal, they checked timetables and changed on to a Bonanza bus heading for Woods Hole, downgrading somewhat as they shunted their bags to a smaller, rustier version of the carriage they had just left, Primrose patting the seat for fleas and then preferring to sit on Herb. As they pulled out on to the coast road, a long weaving link of towns, she dropped her head against his shoulder and sighed contentedly. 'I've got a good feeling about this place,' she told him.

Herb nodded, wishing he could say the same of his legs, quickly numbing beneath her weight.

'Martha's Vineyard, you say?' she asked, a more detailed map bought at the last station giving a little more shape to the green fingernail.

Herb nodded. 'It's probably just a shack, you know. The guy said almost as much.'

Primrose shrugged. 'It's what it's worth to us, that matters.'

'In an ideal world, yes,' Herb countered.

'And who's to say this isn't one?' She smiled at him, smugly, then gazed towards the rolling landscape of beaches and hills beyond the window. 'Looks pretty good to me.'

They arrived at the ferry terminal for the islands just after six, in time for the 7.15 ferry, but a sudden squall across the bay followed by a freak craving of the vegetarian Primrose for lobster, meant they were not actually afloat until some time after ten.

Add to this a vigorous bout of seasickness on the part of
Primrose – guilt over the lobster, no doubt – and the rather dis-
abling queasiness exhibited by Herb, who could not even be in
the same room as someone throwing up, and it was a journey of
some proportions. By the time they eventually reached dry
land – Primrose having secured the sympathies of a local who
offered to drive her ashore, Herb preferring to walk – they were
drained of any other emotion than the desperate urge to sleep.

'Just so, so tired,' Primrose mumbled as she climbed,
then fell out of the car door. waving to her good samaritan.

'Me too,' groaned Herb, as he slowly eased her to her
feet. 'Time we were there.'

They found a taxi on the main street, Herb jogging ahead to check
he was going their way, then climbing wearily into the back.

'Where to?' the T-shirted driver demanded, twisting
around and flicking on his interior light.

'I don't know exactly. I've got papers. Hold on, I'll find
them.' Herb leaned back out the door to gesture to Primrose,
dragging across the road in his wake. 'Papers,' he demanded,
and she handed him her vanity case, watching as Herb rooted
inside then passed the deeds to the driver.

'Hey!' The driver, whose name, Ben, was stitched to the
pocket of his shirt, the work of a still adoring mother, held up
his hands. 'I'm a cab driver, not a lawyer. You give me the
address, I'll get you there. I can't be messing with papers.'

Herb took them back and leaned towards the front,

holding them under the light and pointing with his finger. 'Wenonah's Place,' he indicated. 'Off Moshup's Trail.'

Ben nodded, and flicked off the light, waiting until Primrose was inside the car then reaching back to slam the door. There was silence for a while as the car pulled away from the lights of the dock, twisting through the town, with its white-faced houses and clipped lawns, and edging on to a darker, less welcoming road which was taking them inland. Primrose sat on her hands, twiddling with the folds of worn leather, torn in places to reveal patches of yellow sponge like a ripe Camembert escaping its skin. She squidged a few bits back in, then concentrated on the road.

Ben, however, was less diligent. 'It's Wampanoag land, you know,' he announced, looking back and steering with his knees as he handed them a map. 'Wenonah's not been around for probably five, six years now, but her house was one of the first to get reclaimed.'

Herb shook his head and leaned forward, taking the map but gesturing towards the road. 'Wampa who?' he asked.

'Wampanoag. It's a tribe. Gay Head, where we're headin', was their land. One day soon they'll get it all given back, and then there'll be a different constitution and hell knows what else, casinos, strip joints.' He was turning around again, enjoying the look of horror which had taken over Primrose's previously calm features.

Herb was amused. 'I won a brothel,' he grinned, elbowing Primrose. 'What do you make of that?'

Primrose ignored him, staring out the window. 'Gay Head?' she mused. 'That's a funny name for a place, isn't it?'

Ben smirked, flicking on his wipers to clean the windscreen, then suddenly braking as he realised he had missed the turning. Herb lurched exaggeratedly, then reached for his hither-unworn seatbelt, clicking it fast. 'So what's it like, Wenonah's Place?'

'Far as I know, it's just an old shack right now. The lighthouse guy used to use it for mooring his boat to, and 'til a couple of months back there were three or four hippies from the cliffs sleeping out back. Right now it's empty. There's no one about on the island at this time of year that doesn't have a bed and four walls to hide away in, not unless they're half-crazed.'

While Primrose considered that being out of her mind might be a good thing right now, Herb was on a more literal bent.

'There's a lighthouse?' he asked, the idea of living in the spotlight appealing to him already.

'Course. The Gay Head Light. Quite a landmark if you're twenty miles out to sea. There's talk of a sea monster too, but that's more of a Wampanoag thing: they're kinda big on their monsters. Though I have to say the last guy who reckoned to have seen it came from Ohio, so it's each to their own.' He grinned, and reflected for a moment as he lit a cigarette. 'No one ever knew what happened to Wenonah. She just disappeared one day and never came back. Left her son Johnny an' everything. Weird, don't you think?'

Herb shook his head. 'Picked up on a drugs charge by the New York State police. Jumped bail.'

'You're kidding me?' Ben swivelled almost full circle, the steering-wheel taking a similar turn, and it was only Primrose physically pushing him back to face the road that prevented them hurtling into the ditch.

Herb grinned, and put his chin on the back of Ben's seat. 'Bit of a naughty, girl, Wenonah.' He turned to Primrose, who was white as a sheet and feeling queasy again. 'Having second thoughts yet, Rosie girl? Not too late to go back to Hampstead, you know!'

Primrose forced a smile. 'Are we nearly there?' she wondered, rolling down her window to get some air.

'Not long,' Ben informed her, still impressed by the bail thing. 'Sit back and relax, we've got a bit of a climb when we get there.'

Primrose did as she was told, feeling in her pocket for the deeds to the house and patting them in an attempt at confidence. For a second or two she wondered if reading their future in the lyrics of a song was a habit exceptional to herself, but then she remembered Herb was here too, and let the thought go. 'Exciting, isn't it?' she asked, leaning forwards against his leg, pressing it deeper into the foaming seat.

He nodded. 'I should play poker more often,' he grinned.

It took a good fifty minutes to traverse the island, down to up, and with the extra fifteen or so added for the rather elaborate detour down a neighbouring driveway, it was gone midnight by the time they cut the engine just beyond a grass verge and Ben gestured to them to get out. Primrose sat forward sleepily and stared at the black swilling sky out the window, watching it flash on and off, red then white, under the watchful eye of the lighthouse. All around them the sea roared, and through a crack in the car door, the wind pursed its lips to whistle.

'Do you need the papers?' Primrose asked, reaching forward with the deeds.

Ben pulled a face. 'Do you think there's anyone here who cares?'

She shrugged, looking towards Herb who was out of the car and gazing up at the hiccuping lamp. 'Isn't there?'

Ben walked around to the door, opened it, and helped her out. Then he reached inside, picked up her vanity case, and hooked it over his arm. 'Come on then,' he insisted, looking towards Herb. 'We're not there yet.'

Nor were they there ten minutes later, for Ben was having something of a problem locating the path to get there. 'There's a gate here somewhere,' he promised, fumbling around the waist-high tangles of blackberry bushes and gorse.

'Can we not just get to it from the road?' Herb asked.

Ben snorted. 'Don't you think I'd be doing that if we could? No, the only way is down the cliff path.' Something creaked in the dark night, and Ben raised his hand. 'Got it,' he declared, standing back then kicking some unseen but loudly splintering gate. 'Come on. We've all got homes to get to.'

He stood back, holding out a hand for Primrose then pointing her down the path. 'I've got your bag,' he told her, hoping his diligence would be reflected in the tip. 'Straight down, mind the brambles.'

Primrose hesitated, waiting for Herb to join her, but he was gazing back towards the lighthouse, rubbing his eyes against the red, then white, then red sky. In the distance some-where, a dog howled and a door slammed, and as Herb turned slowly back to them, Ben thumbed towards the sound and named it Jeannie.

'She's got the quahog stall. Lives in her trailer, just the other side. She'll be your nearest neighbour so you'd better keep her sweet.'

'Quahog?' asked Primrose, thinking Dr Seuss.

'Clams,' revealed Ben. 'Go on.' And he pushed first her, then Herb, down the unlit, bramble-tangled path towards the beach.

'So we've got a neighbour then,' Primrose mumbled, catching at a bramble as it flicked into her face.

'Give or take a half-mile,' Ben told her.

Primrose turned back and took Herb's hand, allowing his weight to rush them towards the beach, while Ben fol-lowed carefully behind.

'Left,' he gestured, although they had no choice given the slamming sea and flat hand of cliff which met them on the other side. Herb waited, allowing Ben to lead, then slowly followed him along the pebbled beach, kicking at driftwood and seaweed as it sought to come with them. At his side Primrose was concentrating upon her feet, wearier with every step, and up ahead Ben looked about nervously, not entirely sure that this was right, but as Herb spun circles in the dipping light, he was somewhere quite else. Faster and faster, tripping and turning, pebbles and shells scuffed beneath his feet and landed like confetti all around them, and just as he thought he would spin right off this beach, dizziness hit him a quick right hook and the world went still.

'Shit,' he murmured, lifting himself on to his elbows and opening his eyes. His head still spinning, he waited a moment for the landscape to settle, looking around for the others but finding himself alone. 'Shit,' he repeated, suddenly afraid. Raising himself on to all fours, he crept the two or three yards up the beach that kept him out of the waves, and as panic began to take hold, a hand on his arm pulled him upright and Ben was leading him around the cliffs. And then there it was, rising out of the sand dunes like some great beached whale, a single storey of flat grey shingle eyeing them with distrust as another wave licked its wounds. He sighed in relief, reaching out towards Primrose who was standing at its side, her hand on a fin of deck.

'Wenonah's Place,' Ben announced, letting go of his arm.

Herb nodded, staring at the slipping deck and rotted steps and Primrose staring back at him.

This, then, was home.

Chapter Five

'What do you think?' Primrose waited for Herb to answer, but when he was silent, she looked towards Ben. 'Do you like it?'

Ben shrugged, he too waiting for Herb.

Herb sighed loudly. Or perhaps it was the wind. Primrose raised her hands. 'What then?'

'It's . . .' He hesitated, moving a step or two and peering around the back. 'It's certainly on the beach,' he observed, kicking a small flurry of sand in the general direction of the deck. He glanced at Ben. 'You sure this is the right place, now? This is Wenonah's, off what's-it-called trail, like on the deeds.'

Ben nodded. 'This is it. Look around, you won't find another one within two or three miles.' He glanced towards the cliffs. 'Listen, I'll take you back again, if you like, find you a hotel or something in town if you don't reckon on staying here.' He glanced towards Primrose. 'You've seen the place now, why not make any decisions in daylight?'

'What do you think?' asked Primrose, looking from Herb to the house and back again.

Herb slumped a little lower inside his coat. 'We're here now,' he considered, suddenly tired and unwilling to trek all the way back again. 'Why don't we just stay here for now.'

'Suit yourselves.' Ben fumbled in his pocket and pulled out a slightly crushed box of matches. 'Shouldn't think there'll be any lights working. There's usually a generator to these places that'll need firing up. These'll get you into bed at least.'

Herb took the box with a 'thanks' and handed it to Primrose. 'Come on then,' he urged, testing the front steps with his foot while Primrose swung her arms excitedly. A loud crack, and the railing and two top treads were swinging with her. Herb stood back, thinking, then gestured to Primrose to follow him around the back.

'Have you no key?' Ben wondered, as he watched Herb pick out a piece of driftwood and size it up as a possible door breaker.

'Apparently old Wenonah took them with her when she skipped bail. This'll do.' And he jumped on to the back deck, less exposed than the front and hence better preserved, and batted the wood against the door. With the barest of complaints, it clattered open, and Herb peeped inside.

'I'll see you,' Ben called, heading back towards the cliffs, not wishing to be a part of this venture any more. 'You can pay me tomorrow. I'll call by to see if you need a lift back.'

'Are you sure?' Primrose was suddenly embarrassed. 'I can pay you now if you prefer.'

Ben waved dismissively. 'Tomorrow,' he told her, pointing around the front to where he had left her case. 'Sleep well.'

Inside, Herb was looking for a light switch. Feeling along the walls, his fingers slipped across squares of loose paper, damp and smooth with corners that curled, and when he lit a match he saw sheet upon sheet of newspaper lining the room. Black and white photographs stared at him from the shadows, and he called Primrose, lighting a second match and handing it to her, wondering what it all meant. Certain of the pages were circled in ink, names picked out, photographs drawn upon, and for some time they could do nothing but stare, lighting new matches as old ones burned down, lost in that overwritten room.

'Look.' Primrose pointed to a table in the centre of the room, covered in piles of blank paper, weighted down with rocks. In the middle of them all, a large black typewriter sat majestic and stern, several keys stuck in the depressed position, rust or salt presumably the culprit. 'Do you think Wenonah was a writer too?' Primrose wondered.

Herb shrugged.

'Come on.' Primrose lit another match and pulled him towards the shadow of a door on the opposite side of the room, which led to a smaller space, a hallway, off which led three further doors. Opening one, Primrose could just make out the hunched shoulders of an armchair. 'Drawing room,' she announced.

'Lounge,' corrected Herb.

She leant upon the second door. A fridge sat fat and open just inside, gleaming white and luminous in the dim room. 'Kitchen,' she told him, waiting for his alternative, but none came.

And then she opened the third. Taking a step inside, the match she was holding flickered and went out, a draught from somewhere above their heads catching it and preventing her from lighting another one. She sighed and dropped the box, looking up towards the draught just as the lamp on the cliffs above swung their way and the room was briefly lit up, then fell dark again. Pulling Herb into the room with her, she waited fifteen seconds or so, then grinned as the light came by again, this time red. 'There must be a hole in the roof,' she suggested. 'Or a window open.'

Herb nodded, repeating the gesture for Primrose's benefit with the next swing of the lamp. He yawned, loudly and indulgently. 'I'm knackered,' he breathed, seeing the bed turn rosy in the centre of the room then disappear again. 'Let's just get some sleep. There's no point poking around this place until we can see what we're doing.'

Primrose murmured in agreement, nevertheless still gazing around, piecing the room together in a jigsaw of glimpses. 'Have you seen the walls in here?' she asked, all four of them patchworked with hundreds and hundreds of post-cards, picture side up. 'How many do you think there are?'

'No idea,' sighed Herb, still yawning. 'But I'm getting some sleep now, so you can count them by yourself if you're that way inclined.' He stumbled towards where he remem-bered seeing the bed, falling on to it and closing his eyes just as the room turned bright again. Primrose followed him, feeling for his legs, arms, chest, then fitting herself alongside.

'Our first night in our own bed,' Primrose told him, wrapping her arms about his body and hugging tight.

'Except it's not really ours,' Herb told her. He was silent for a moment. 'Can you smell something strange in here?'

'I think it's just a bit musty. The whole place probably needs a good airing.'

'Maybe,' breathed Herb, sinking lower into the tickling eiderdown, and sneezing exhaustedly. Moving Primrose's plait from where it had fallen across his cheek, he rolled on to his side, holding her arm as she held him. 'Night then,' he mur-mured, pulling his jacket over them as a gust of wind caught the bed.

'Night,' returned Primrose. 'Welcome home.'

They were woken just before dawn by a heavy weight landing with a thud at the end of the bed. Primrose shot upright, her first thought being for the absconding Wenonah, back to resume possession, but when this initial landing was followed

by a second and then a third, until the whole end of the mattress dipped almost to the floor, she quickly promoted
Wenonah to a tribe of marauding locals and started screaming
for mercy. Herb, thus long awake but taking his time to get a
grip on things, yanked his coat over her head as if she were a
dog he wanted to stop barking, then sat up, asking, as bravely
as he could, 'Who's there?'

Silence. The thuds on the bed, still there judging by the
dip, did not move. Waiting for the inevitable swoop of light,
Herb crouched back against the wall – Primrose shaking somewhere around his right knee – feeling around the floor at the
side of the bed for something to defend them with. But all his
fingers met was soft, large clumps of what felt like feathers
attaching themselves to his sleeves and wristwatch, and he
jerked back his hand just as the lamp swung around. Two child-
sized figures were hunched at the end of the bed, the third by
the door, and as Herb craned forward, distrusting his eyes, the
room went dark again.

'Who is it?' Primrose whispered, from beneath his coat.
Herb did not respond. 'Who is it?' she repeated, louder, this
time addressing the intruders.

Nobody moved. Then as Primrose gradually peeled back
the shell of Herb's coat, deciding that a piece of gabardine
would be of little defence anyway, the lamp swung white across
the opening in the roof and the shapes at the end of the bed
began to squawk.

'Turkeys?' Primrose gasped, turning to face Herb.

Herb was silent, vaguely suspecting this whole thing to be a dream and waiting for it to pass.

'My God, turkeys!' Primrose repeated, leaning forward and squinting as her eyes gradually adjusted to the dark. She reached towards the smaller of the two still perched on the end of the bed. It stared at her, shuffling sideways, then jumped for the door. Primrose jumped after it, a flurry of feathers and wings escaping in front of her, disappearing out into the hall with a crash and a clatter, then gone.

'They were turkeys,' she told Herb disbelievingly. 'On our bed.' She looked up, towards the hole above them through which they had clearly arrived, and shook her head in confusion. 'Where can they have come from?'

'The roof, presumably,' Herb mumbled, his only and most helpful comment so far.

'But where . . .?' Primrose sat down on the bed and gazed upwards, the black sky above seeming to lighten even as she watched, and as the room paled to the colour of weak tea, she was shivering.

'Take my coat,' Herb offered, handing back her shroud and moving away from the wall to which he had been pressed. As he did so, another bird dropped through the hole, landing on the bed between them then screeching loudly as Herb jumped backwards with a curse. Seconds later it was followed by another bird, and then another, falling like small missiles on the bed and surrounding rugs and sending a flurry of feathers rising in their wake, until they had counted a further six to add

to the original three, and the numbers seemed no longer rel-
evant. Once again the turkeys disappeared out the door, into
the hall, and were gone, the spluttering of the screen door out
back suggesting it was the dunes they had headed for, and as
the room was their own again, bright now with the translucent
light of morning, Herb tipped off the end of the bed on to his
knees and began to moan. 'Jesus Christ, Jesus Christ, Jesus
Christ,' he told the mattress, his face sunk in feathers and
coats. 'What in God's heaven was that?'

Herb had given up on religion around the same time as he had
given up on Ireland, but that night, when all those turkeys
threw themselves on to the bed, cascading towards him like an
Old Testament plague, something of his old faith returned to
him.

'They were just birds,' Primrose told him, as he knelt by
the side of the bed, shaking inconsolably.

'I know, I know,' he mumbled, refusing to look up.

And he was still there, trembling, two hours later, after
Primrose had filled two pillowcases with the handfuls of feathers she was collecting from the floor and bed. And still there
another hour after that, when she had worked her way around
the outside of the house, levering off shutters and storm windows with the driftwood they had made such good use of the
night before. 'Just birds, I know,' he answered, when she came
to sit by his head, stroking his hair and gently urging him to get
up, to see what she had done. 'I know, I know.'

When Ben arrived around nine, climbing up the back steps and appearing in the laundry room with armfuls of blankets and a steaming flask, the house was silent. Glancing around at the newspapered walls and paper-sunken desk, he rolled his eyes in amusement, then leaned back to the now defunct screen door and knocked loudly.

'Anyone there?' he called, peering back out to the deck, then moving towards the hall. 'You guys okay?' A rustling in the next room confirmed their presence, and he waited a moment. 'Hello?'

'Hi.' Primrose appeared in the doorway, a bulging pillowcase hanging from one hand, and put her fingers to her lips. 'Herb's sleeping,' she whispered.

'Oh,' Ben mouthed.

'Come into the kitchen.' Relieving him of the flask, she led him towards the room with the fridge, looking back to check he was following. 'It's rather eccentric, isn't it?' she smiled.

Ben grinned, shaking his head as he swivelled around to take in the mosaiced surfaces of every wall, the hall all rosebuds and greeting cards, the kitchen a more sombre effort with its shopping lists and recipes chalked across the blackboard painted walls.

'Is this the first time you've been inside?' Primrose asked.

Ben gestured to her to open the flask, gratefully taking the lid of coffee she handed to him. 'Yeah,' he breathed. 'She was kind of a quiet one, Wenonah.' He ran his finger across one of the chalked recipes, streaking a dusty line through three eggs and a cup of sugar.

Primrose nodded, searching the cupboards for another cup but finding only stacks of old newspapers and the odd feather. She picked up the latter and shoved them into the pillowcase, holding it open to show Ben. 'Turkeys,' she told him, pointing towards the bedroom. 'There were turkeys coming through the roof.'

'They're a real problem up here. Wild ones, you know, just roaming about the lanes. Probably like this place because no one's been here for so long. You need to get yourselves a shotgun or something if you're planning on staying around.'

Primrose looked horrified. 'They're dangerous?' she asked.

'No, tame as anything. But they'll have all the shingles off the house soon as look at it, and they make bombsites of gardens.'

Primrose glanced out the window at the gleaming beach and wondered where he expected her to find a garden. 'But they're not dangerous?' she repeated.

'No. Just a nuisance.'

Primrose pulled a face. She could live with nuisances. 'I think we just need to get the holes fixed,' she told him, 'the holes they fell through. There's a big one in the ceiling, then a bigger one in the roof. They've obviously had quite a party up there.'

'Party animals,' Ben quipped, feeling in his pocket for the

Tupperware of sausage pancakes he had made before he came out. 'I made these for you,' he offered. 'Pigs in blankets. Thought you'd be hungry for a bite.'

Primrose took them, grateful for the thought if not the pigs. 'Herb will eat them,' she told him, glancing towards the bedroom. 'When he wakes up. I think he found it all a bit of a shock.' Standing back, she studied the newspaper-stacked cupboards and the empty fridge and rubbed her head, still searching for a cup.

'Try the oven,' Ben suggested, this being the only place left.

Wrenching open the rusting door, Primrose surveyed the piles of plates and mugs that filled the two shelves. 'How did you know she'd keep them in the oven? Is that normal around here?'

'It was a guess. Here.' He handed her the flask, watching her pour two mugs of coffee and set one to the side. 'So you going to get him up on the roof later?'

'Herb? Maybe.' Primrose took a slurp of coffee, then reconsidered. Whatever illusions she might or might not have about Herb, even she could not see him with a tool-box in his hands. 'Perhaps it would be better just to get someone in.'

Ben looked away, his own helpfulness limited to non-labouring favours, then had an idea. 'I know just the guy for you,' he grinned, glancing towards the door as a fit of sneezing announced Herb's awakening. Primrose looked with him, reaching for the second mug of coffee and moving towards the hall. 'Have you sorted in no time, Johnson will. I'll get him to come round.'

Johnson 'just the guy' Macgregor, or Johnny as he preferred to be known, was Wenonah's son, the result of a one-night stand with a blues guitarist from Kentucky whose name she decided to keep but whose presence she had never found much use for. From the day Johnny was born she had taught him that women stick around and make ends meet, whereas men meet their ends and disappear, and although this didn't stop her letting the odd one stop over, they were cleared away with the breakfast things and rarely seen again. Johnny soon came to regard them as just another brand of cereal, interesting at first glance, but always the same old offer on the back, and as the years went by he stopped hoping for one of them to introduce himself as his father, and concentrated on the toast instead. When, aged sixteen, he woke up one morning to discover his mother had left home with one such cornflake, a particularly unsavoury character for whom she would end up wanted in eleven states, it seemed only to prove his point. Only Jeannie, the quahog lady, offered any kind of consolation, whipping him up a plate of eggs and introducing the concept of brunch, but when she turned out to be planning menus of a different kind, his native good looks and musical hands attracting many a surrogate mother, he decided he was better off alone. Within days he had closed up the house, moving down the bay to a disused boatshed more suited to his needs, and with his life now a cycle of mowing lawns in the summer and mending nets when it got cold, it was only the turkeys he missed.

The turkeys. His mother, who gave him the Indian name Chasing Eagle but secretly preferred her birds to be of a less predatory nature, had long considered the Vineyard's flock of wild turkeys to be something of a vocation, and under her watchful eye they had been fed, watered, and even given a roof over their heads when the weather was especially chill, as she hated to think of them sleeping rough. For years he had lain awake on the couch, listening to them scratching and gobbling around the bedroom, and one of the last things he had done before he moved out was loosen a few shingles so they could still get in if it snowed. It was thus no surprise to him when Ben called by, asking if he might mend the roof and help with some turkey clearing.

'Ma's birds still hanging about then?'

'Yeah, I told Primrose – that's her name, the new lady – she'd do best just to buy a big gun, but she figured she'd fix up the roof instead.'

Johnny nodded approvingly. And while he felt no obligation to the house or its new owners – the fact that his mother had put the place up as a bail bond had kind of finished the deal for him – he figured he owed it to the turkeys to do what he could.

'I'll swing by later on,' he told Ben, 'see what I can do.'

Ben grinned, miming a shotgun in recognition of the alternatives, and patted Johnny's head. 'You're a good kid.'

'I'll see what I can do,' Johnny repeated, waving as he tugged closed the double doors of the boatshed and stepped over the sofa into his dinghy. One leg inside the boat, the other braced against his sitting-room wall, he pushed the boat down the length of the shed, water lapping at the far end, slid back the water gate, and rowed out on to Squibnocket Pond. Aiming for the creek then out into the Sound, Johnny pulled his sweater high about his ears, dipped his head, and made for home.

Chapter Six

Despite his initial readiness it took Johnny four days to reach the house, each time he saw the cliffs just before the house, turning back again. In the end, Ben drove back down there and picked him up in the taxi, driving him to the lighthouse and walking him down the cliff path himself, and even then Johnny would have made a run for it had Primrose not met them on the beach. But when he saw her there still wearing the yellow dress and purple tights she had travelled in, her face and hands black from scrubbing at walls, he could think only of following, and as she led the familiar way up the sands to the house, he was as tame as the turkeys he had come to save.

'So you're Johnny.' As they reached the house, Primrose turned around and took his hand, directing him towards the back. 'The front steps are a little unpredictable,' she told him. 'Although I suppose you already know that.'

'They, er, they need a bit of attention, I guess,' he mumbled. 'You want me to take a look.'

Primrose smiled politely, but gestured towards the roof. 'Would you mind really if we did the roof first? We've been lucky the last few days, but if it rains . . .'

'It won't rain,' Johnny told her, glancing at the sky. Nevertheless, he hoisted himself on to the back railing and eased on to the sloping roof, striding towards the centre and stopping as he reached the hole. 'You met Theresa and the family, then,' he called back, leaning out towards the dunes to catch Primrose's eye. 'The turkeys,' he clarified, when she seemed confused.

'Oh, yes. They introduced themselves the first night we were here.' She glanced towards the laundry room where Herb was working his way around the walls, reading the scraps of newspaper stuck there and every so often quoting from articles he found particularly interesting. 'We've been sleeping in the sitting-room ever since.'

Johnny considered the hole, then returned to the edge of the roof and jumped down. 'Won't take long,' he reassured, catching sight of Herb through the laundry window just as Herb noticed him go flying past. 'I'll be back tomorrow with some tools.'

Primrose held up her hand, loath to wait another four days before she might sleep in her bed. 'We've got tools,' she offered, Ben having brought a set around the day before when things were getting desperate. 'Could you not have a go at it today?'

Johnny considered. 'You got some coffee?'

'Tea?'

He thought for a moment. 'Okay.' He hoiked himself back on to the roof, and scratched his neck distractedly. 'But I'm not promising anything. I'll just see what I can do.'

Used to men and their lack of promises, Primrose held up her hands in acceptance, and went to boil the kettle. As she did so, Herb appeared in the doorway, the knees of his jeans still stuck with feathers from his impromptu but frequent kneelings, and handed her an article on the lighthouse.

'You know it's all electric,' he told her, pointing through the window towards the cliffs. 'Has been since '52.'

Primrose nodded. 'Otherwise we'd have two neighbours, Jeannie and the lighthouse keeper.' She busied herself taking cups and saucers out of the oven, placing them on a tray she had found out back and adding a handful of spoons. 'Johnny, Wenonah's son, is here to mend the roof. Did you see him just now?'

'Is that the one just fell past the window?'

'Yes.'

Herb shook his head. 'Didn't really get a look. You know,' he held his hand out for the cutting and considered it for a moment, 'she was quite a character, this Wenonah.' He

pointed to the fading photograph of the lighthouse, then used
the drawing pin which had fixed it to the wall to push back his
cuticles. 'Apart from those bloody birds, I think I could have
been quite fond of her.' He turned and wandered back to the
laundry room, leaving Primrose staring at the boiled kettle
and trying to remember where she'd put the cups.

When she next saw Herb, he was standing on the bed looking
up through the hole in the roof and gazing at Johnny as he
drank the tea she had just made him. 'Did you want a cup,
Herb?' she asked, leaning against the doorway and picking a
feather from where it had lodged in the plasterwork. He shook
his head. 'Are you worried about the turkeys? You know they
only come through at night.' He shook his head again. She
approached the bed, perching on the end and joining him in his
staring.

   Just beyond the hole, Johnny sat fiddling with a piece of
slate he was trying to fix back into place. The late afternoon
sun bounced off his shoulders and hair, filling the sky with
golden light, and as Primrose glanced at Herb's upturned face
she saw it was similarly glowing. 'You've met then,' she noted,
clearing her throat and waving when Johnny turned around.
'He seems to be doing a good job, doesn't he?'

   'What did you say his name was?'

   'Johnny, Johnny Macgregor, Wenonah's son, a friend of
Ben's.' Primrose reached towards Herb and caught his chin in
her fingers, pulling his face down and watching the light drain

away like water through a plughole. 'Are you all right, Herb?' she asked, feeling his forehead with the flat of her hand, then feeling her own in comparison. 'Do you think you should lie down?'

'Maybe.'

And so Herb lay down, prostrate beneath the ever-diminishing hole in the roof, while Primrose laid wet flannels across his forehead and coaxed him to drink tea, and it was only when night fell, and the view was replaced by the waddling bellies of the ever more at-home turkeys, that he seemed to revive a little.

'Do you want me to call a doctor?' Primrose checked, once again feeling his brow.

Herb shook his head. 'There's a lot of work needs doing around here then?' he mused, glancing about the dulling room.

'I suppose so, but we're not in any rush.'

'Good. Good.' And he nodded appreciatively towards the hole in the roof. 'I'm feeling better already.'

When Johnny arrived the next morning, then, he had his work cut out for him. Rebuilding decks, mending railings, painting window frames, unblocking sinks; this was only the beginning, and in the weeks that followed they none of them could do enough for each other. As the seas got rougher and the weather turned towards winter, Herb would even offer to walk him home, suggesting it was madness to tempt the Atlantic the way he did, but Johnny never took him up on this.

He preferred to go his own way, perhaps with a pie or casserole Primrose had cooked from one of his mother's recipes chalked to the wall, sometimes just with his thoughts. But as the house began to lift itself up out of the declining sands, standing a little stronger in the few places upon which it still had purchase, they could all admit to feeling increasingly at home.

'It makes it all so worthwhile, doesn't it?' Primrose declared, one rainy evening as they stood on the deck watching Johnny disappear beneath the shadows of the cliffs.

And Herb nodded resolutely, his face flashing on and off in the beam of the lighthouse, and led her inside.

It was Johnny's idea that Primrose put her cooking skills to some greater purpose than just lunch, her versions of Wenonah's blackboard specials far surpassing the originals. Of particular note were her pies, a triumphant combination of Primrose's own pastry recipe, learned on a summer cookery course in Holland Park, and the local produce Johnny went out of his way to introduce her to, and when a crop of late beach-plums served as the basis for one of the best meals he had ever eaten, he could no longer hold back.

'You gotta start a business,' he told her, taking her hand and sitting her down. 'This is just too good to waste on us alone.'

'It's not wasted. You two enjoy it, don't you? There's no need for it to be anything more.'

'But this place is crying out for good food. Good basic local cooking.' The same entrepreneurial spirit that had led his mother to be picked up on a drugs charge sparked in Johnny now. 'I'll help you set up, of course. Introduce you to a couple of people I know. But I'm telling you, come summertime these beaches are heaving. You get yourself a licence and we're laughing.'

'He's right, you know,' Herb agreed, taking another mouthful of pie and grinning pastry. 'He's on to something.'

Primrose frowned. But because there had been no other bids to fund their lifestyle, and given her savings account was getting smaller by the day, she had no choice but to agree. With a promise from Herb that he would also start work, his much talked about but as yet unstarted novel falling victim to his preferred activities of trailing after Johnny and reading the wallpaper, she agreed to making a few test pies and left it at that. Then she gathered up the few scraps they had left, dropped them into a bowl in which she had collected ends of bread and vegetable peelings, and went outside to give the turkeys their supper.

Over the next few weeks the house was a hive of industry, Herb true to his word, tucking himself deep inside the laundry room with a copy of Agatha Christie and an ambition for better things, and Primrose wiping herself a clean corner of the blackboard and setting to work on her pies. Johnny Macgregor finished off his list of jobs then joined Primrose in the kitchen, occasionally bringing along some nets he was mending, and adding a fug of his own to the already steaming room. And there they would sit, perhaps discussing plans to redecorate the sitting-room, sometimes just sitting, and on the few occasions Herb joined them there, slamming a few doors to make his presence felt, they would grin and pass him pie or net as the occasion required.

And so their lives took shape, Herb, Primrose and Johnny Macgregor, each in their own way fulfilled. Christmas came and went, a small affair with a couple of candles in the window and a long tearful call to Primrose's parents on the telephone they had put in only the week before. With a rather pitiful attempt at 'Away in a Manger' to the beat of a wooden spoon on Herb's typewriter – the most action it had seen in weeks – and a vegetarian turkey fashioned from soya beans and seaweed, they slipped into the new year as haplessly as they had fallen out of the last one.

'What are your resolutions?' Primrose asked, head to head with Herb across one of her toilet roll and tissue paper Christmas crackers.

Herb shrugged. 'Stay lucky, I guess.'

Primrose agreed. 'Mine too. And start doing something with all these pies,' she added, gesturing to the corner where stacks of her experiments tottered drunkenly. She had stopped being quite so generous with the turkeys' supper since one had appeared beside her in the bath one night, obesity preventing it from flying on to the roof as usual and forcing a pit stop through the bathroom window instead.

'I'm with you there,' Johnny agreed.

And thus they toasted 1970 and hoped for a good one. A couple of pies each just to clear the backlog, and as January brought snow and February much of the same, Johnny Macgregor went back to his boatshed to await calmer seas, and Herb and Primrose bedded down with the turkeys and wondered at their ever-expanding waistlines and the increasing lateness of spring.

Chapter Seven

First they got fat, and then Primrose got fatter, and then she got fatter still. And despite no longer tasting her experiments and a new regime of seaweed broths and coleslaw brought in to take the edge off the winter insulation, her belly simply kept growing, until some time around Easter, plump and golden like one of her pies, somebody predicted a girl.

Primrose had been hanging around the deck all afternoon, 'boondoggling' as Johnny called it, watching shells spin helter skelter in the wind and counting seagulls, and she was just about to make herself her fourth cup of tea that day when a figure further down the beach caught her eye and she waited, always glad of a little company. As the figure came closer, she saw it was Jeannie the quahog lady, presumably looking for

Johnny, and Primrose began to wave, gesturing he was not here today, then wandered inside.

When she returned, teapot in hand, Jeannie was sitting on the deck, feet on the railings. 'Hiya,' she smiled. 'You read my mind.'

'Cup of tea?' asked Primrose.

'Sure do,' replied Jeannie, who increasingly resembled the clams she was famous for, with her sallow skin and puffed-out cheeks. 'If you'll make it a black coffee, one sugar.'

'Course,' Primrose smiled, turning and walking back through the screen door with her teapot. Two minutes later she was back with two mugs of coffee.

'So how you doin'?' Jeannie demanded, reaching into her smock pocket for her cigarettes, then lighting one against the wind. 'Blooming, I see.'

Primrose nodded self-consciously. 'I've always fluctu-ated,' she murmured, clearing a space on the table for their mugs. 'It's my metabolism.'

'My Eliot was under my ribs almost from day one, poking out like a pot handle, always getting in the way. Still exactly the same now, probably what started it. Not like that neat little thing you've got – I'm betting anything you want that's a girl hiding out in there. Girls tuck 'emselves in all tidy, nice and low. You remember now it was me said she's a girl.'

Primrose stared at her, then patted her belly. And just as she was about to start once again on the fluctuating metabo-lism number, a strange fluttering, rather like a fish flipping

somersaults deep inside her, distracted her, and she instead sat
down. 'You think I'm pregnant,' she whispered, voice shaking.
She stared out to sea where a small boat scuppered across the
horizon, sail flapping like knickers on a washing line. She
pulled at the tight band of elastic which dug ridges around her
belly, and snapped it distractedly. 'I'm pregnant,' she
repeated, this time in confirmation. 'Oh, my God, of course.
I'm not fat. I'm pregnant. I'm going to have a baby. I'm going
to have a girl.'

When Herb got home from The Bunch of Grapes bookstore
later that evening (his favourite hangout these days, second to
Johnny), she was still sitting there, sipping her cold coffee and
repeating the words over and over. Jeannie had made herself
scarce two or three hours before, finding it all a bit weird, this
pretending not to know business, and as Herb climbed the
steps he almost mistook her for a turkey, all hunched and
chuntering and rather in the way. 'Are you all right?' he asked,
squinting at her across the darkness. 'Why didn't you switch
on any of the lights?'

'We're going to have a girl,' Primrose declared, moon-
ing at him over her coffee cup and smiling just that little bit
too much.

'What on earth are you talking about?' he demanded,
lifting her mug and sniffing it suspiciously to check she had not
been at Johnny's boatshed brews again. 'What have you been
up to, Primrose?'

Primrose gazed at him, her eyes filling with fat, watery tears. 'Me,' she mumbled, still smiling, 'me? Nothing. Why?'

It was not surprising that pregnancy came as something of a shock, given that virtually the only activity their bed had seen since they had arrived could be traced to nine clumsy turkeys falling through the roof. Virtually. For there was always the uncomfortable skirmish Primrose had initiated on the occasion of their one-week anniversary, an event both of them regretted after one of the pillowcases of feathers was set loose in the fray and they spent the rest of the night sneezing and trying to retrieve them. Thereafter Primrose settled for a quick cuddle and a well-laced Irish coffee, blaming tiredness and the 'troubles' for the subsequent lack of inter-border relations. In time she came to forget the issue altogether, falling asleep with a trashy paperback much as she had ever done, and when her periods stopped for a couple of months, she assumed her body had forgotten too.

Thus Jeannie and her 'girl' was a shock to the system in more ways than one, although it was a relief to discover she would not be wearing her bellbottoms the wrong way round for ever, and as she took down a couple of Wenonah's post-cards from the bedroom wall and used them to write home, she was beaming from cheek to cheek.

If there was ever a woman born to breed it was Primrose. From the moment she discovered that the 'fluctuations' she so liked to point out were only going one way, she threw out the coleslaw, pulled down the strands of seaweed she had left to dry above Herb's desk in the laundry room, and set to work getting fat. Offering a running commentary upon her changing dress size – both American and European – she was forever stopping strangers on the beach and demanding they guess how many pounds she had put on, adding a couple extra to the scales for dramatic effect. And when she was done with them guessing and done with their 'wows', she invariably dragged them up to the deck to taste her latest pies and sent them back to their beachtowels happy. These were formative times for Primrose, and as Herb sank ever deeper into the newspapered haven of the laundry room, doing nesting of his own, it was the best way she knew how.

Having read something about heightened sensitivity during pregnancy, Primrose had taken her pies to new extremes, putting aside all her previous, more predictable combinations, and deciding to play around. Cranberry and pea one day, apple and sweet potato the next, each cleverly disguised beneath a perfect crust, all golden and glazed and marked with a P (for Primrose, or Pie, or Pastry, she never revealed), and chalked up on the kitchen wall with comments and improvements alongside. She became something of an institution, wandering up and down the beach with her pies making guinea pigs of the summer's first recruits, and as word began to get around and the number of bathers began to swell around lunch, it was only a matter of time and good management before the business took off.

'I've made you a business plan,' Johnny announced one May morning as Primrose was drinking tea on the deck. 'I've done a five-year forecast and a graph of expected profits. I've even thought of a name, if you like it.' He paused, thinking how she seemed to have grown overnight. 'The Wild Turkey Café. What do you think?'

'But we're not a café,' Primrose corrected.

'Doesn't matter. It sounds more professional if there's a suggestion of premises. Trust me.'

Because, as a matter of course, Primrose trusted everyone, she nodded. 'I'll ask Herb,' she told him, disappearing indoors. Minutes later she was back again. 'Whatever,' she repeated, only more enthusiastically. 'So I suppose The Wild Turkey Café it is.'

She sat down on the deck and flicked through Johnny's elaborate business plan, written the night before on Wenonah's old typewriter. (Herb had replaced it with an electric version within weeks of starting work, blaming the former's lack of speed for the little he had to show for himself.) 'You'll do this with me, won't you?' she checked. 'Be my business partner.'

'If you like.'

'I do,' declared Primrose. And as Johnny disappeared to negotiate a settlement with Jeannie, who regarded the beach as her patch despite the fact that most of them were vegetarians who would have nothing to do with clam-faces, Primrose set to work on a seaweed and sorrel recipe which she was convinced had the makings of a classic. They were heady times,

those first months of business – largely due to the hallucino-
genic quality of the seaweed she was using – and as Herb
rewrote Chapter One of his novel, and Johnny designed a logo
for their labels, Primrose sat back and watched her belly, waiting for it to rise.

Given the unpredictable turns her life had taken in recent
months, it was perhaps only natural that she should be drawn
to join an astrology evening class, always keen for a few more
expectations to live up to, and determined to be ready for
them next time. But when she turned up the first night, a
little late because the head had engaged only that morning and
walking was proving something of an obstacle, the class had
finished their analysis of Pisces, her sign, and were working
their way across the chart. Hesitating in the doorway, listening to what a great week Ariens could expect, she debated
whether to stay or go, but when she saw a note on the door
opposite announcing a 'Heal-Thy-Soul' yoga class starting in
fifteen minutes, she simply swapped instead. Hence when
Judith, the yoga instructor, arrived ten minutes later, she
found a new pupil in the heavily pregnant Primrose, stripped
to just her elasticless purple tights and one of Herb's summer
vests, and as enrolment forms flew in one direction and
Primrose's belly stuck fast in the other, acceptance was all.

'Have you done yoga before?' Judith asked, leading her to
a pile of mats and berthing her there like some tanker in the
dock.

Primrose shook her head. 'But I'm a fast learner,' a cramp in her pelvis adding a wheeze to this last.

Judith smiled and batted long eyelashes. 'Strictly speaking, we don't encourage beginners at this late stage' (whether she was referring to Primrose's pregnancy or the fact that they were mid-term was not clear), 'but because I never turn anyone away, you can stay for today.'

Primrose nodded gratefully, another cramp catching her by surprise and tipping her forward on to her face. Somewhere behind her, Judith was demonstrating the half-lotus, and Primrose lay there, listening, until another spasm of pain racked her body, and she began to pant.

'What position is that exactly?' Judith asked, appearing behind her.

'Half-lotus?' wondered Primrose, biting down hard on four layers of sponge.

Judith considered for a moment, then leaned down, putting her mouth next to Primrose's ear. 'Is there something you want to tell me?' she asked, as if Primrose was intending to keep the matter a secret.

Primrose turned her head to face her, all confusion, and attempted to sit up. But halfway up she stopped, gasping as blowtorches burnt gaping holes from her back through to her pelvis, and as she swung there on all fours, she gave up any rights to a soul, healed or otherwise, and calmly, quietly, began to retch.

Primrose threw up constantly for almost four hours,

during which time her classmates had done a crash course in
midwifery from a textbook in the biology room and mastered
a whole series of positions they had not even known existed.
Agatha's ultimate arrival was to the chorus of twenty women
in leotards panting wildly, crouched on all sides, and as she was
passed, screaming, from one bangled pair of hands to the next,
there was no suggestion that there might be someone missing
in all this. It was only when Herb arrived, just after midnight,
worried that her astrology class might have put her off course,
that it occurred to anyone they might have called him. But it
was too late then.

'Oh, God,' he breathed, standing in the doorway and
staring at the muddle of heaving breasts and legwarmers that
met him there. 'Oh, God,' he repeated, when Primrose
offered up his daughter, struggling for a smile and murmuring
something about calling her Yogini, for obvious reasons. And
'Oh, God,' he concluded, when, reaching for the child, he
lifted her out of that circle of vicarious lactation and whisked
her towards the door.

'We'll call her Agatha,' he declared, whipping a copy of
Dial M for Murder out of his jacket pocket and waving it at the
assembled audience, adding 'after Agatha Christie,' just in case
the point had been missed. Lifting the child to his face, he
gently kissed her forehead, resting his cheek on her pulsing
crown, before turning back to the room and announcing they
were leaving. Waiting just long enough for Primrose to pull
herself to her feet and inch after him, he tucked Agatha deep

inside the collar of his summer jacket and moved out into the schoolyard. Suggesting Primrose accept Judith's offer of a ride home and her too tired to argue, he helped her into the back door of the car then quietly, carefully, he and Agatha began the slow walk home, haphazardly followed by half a dozen surrogate mothers not quite ready to let go.

'Look at you,' he murmured, wandering along the grass verge towards the cliffs. But Agatha was sleeping, exhausted by her entrance into this squealing, jangling world, and was looking nowhere. 'We are going to have so much fun,' he promised, a sense of ownership such as he had only ever aspired to suddenly suffusing his body. 'You and me, kiddo. We're going to be a team.'

When he reached the beach, Primrose was waiting for him, rocking from one foot to the other, sore and tired, and wondering where he had been.

'I was showing her the lighthouse,' he told her, neglecting to mention he had climbed up the far side and danced around the lamp walkway in the hope that it might instil in Agatha his love of all things bright and glittering. 'I think she liked it too.'

'Can I take her?' Empty inside, Primrose had more than her usual gaps to fill. 'I've missed her so much.' She reached for Agatha and held the baby tight against her, breathing the soft mixture of Agatha's unbathed muzziness and Herb's ever-overpowering Old Spice.

'I think she missed you too,' Herb noted, pointing to

the patch of wet on his shirt where Agatha had been sucking on it.

Primrose nodded, gazing at her daughter.

'Are you hungry?' Herb wondered, trailing along behind as Primrose hobbled back towards the house. 'I could make us some eggs or something.'

Primrose looked up as she reached the steps, as if surprised to still find him there. 'No, no,' she mumbled, shaking her head. 'I think we'll just sleep. You look after yourself. We'll just sleep.'

She leaned against the screen door and fell through, edging around the table and making straight for the bedroom without turning on a light. Dropping on to the bed, she held Agatha in one arm while she swept books and bedclothes on to the floor – the evidence of Herb's day spent in bed reading crime novels – then levered herself around the child and fell immediately asleep. Herb stood alone and lonely in the kitchen, daughters he could swing around lighthouses never something he had planned upon. And as the enormity of the day swept over him, he ached into a chair, rested his head upon the eggs he had been planning to scramble, and wondered (for the first time with any real seriousness) just quite what all this had to do with a restaurant called Keats and a one-way ticket to New York.

Chapter Eight

Herb had never had something so completely his own as Agatha. When one of Primrose's yoga class dropped round a snapshot she had taken of the baby just minutes after she had been born, all mauve and crinkly, he was so moved by the absolute perfection of this 5″ × 7″ piece of Kodak paper that for days he would not let it out of his sight. Tucking it between the T and Y of his keyboard, he wondered that his life had had meaning without it, and as he was slowly trusted to look after the noisier, less glossy version of this picture, he realised that it hadn't.

'So special,' he would murmur, spinning her in circles around the rustling walls of his laundry room study. 'So mine and so perfect. So special.'

With Primrose hovering in the background, fussing about muslin cloths and insisting he wash his hands before touching her, Herb whispered promises of angels and told her his dreams.

'It's going to be so fine, me and you,' he murmured, nuzzling her squalling face and ignoring Primrose's insistence that the child was hungry. 'Just you wait and see. We're going to be great.'

Reluctantly, he gave her up to the arms of her mother, and wandered towards the laundry room. Minutes later he was back again, pulling on his boots, and as he sprinted out of the house and along the beach, Primrose never even noticed he had gone. When he returned around supper time, his arms full of new Agatha Christies as a tribute to her namesake, in his rucksack a set of feeding bottles he had borrowed from Jeannie, he seized his daughter from the crib Primrose had settled her in, and disappeared to his room.

'Come and help Daddy work,' he mumbled, setting her inside the tin washing tub he had been using for scrap paper. And when Agatha simply closed her eyes and drifted straight back to sleep, he made a note of her loyalty and pushed her beneath the desk. Some time later when Primrose came to find her, he had one leg resting on the desk, the other a crossbar to the bucket, but when she attempted to return her to her newly primped crib, he made such a fuss about paternity rights it was easier to let her stay.

And so Primrose went to bed alone, leaving Herb and

Agatha tap-tapping out the night in the laundry, and as she listened to the scratching of the turkeys above her head, she
decided it was time Herb had distractions of his own, and
determined to find him a job.

She did not have to look far. 'Annual Reports,' declared Johnny
Macgregor, barely had she even touched upon the subject.
'They haven't had anyone do it properly around here since Ma
disappeared, and last year there were two or three people who
got missed off the register. Annual Reports, that's what he
should be doing. It's the perfect solution.' He nodded, handing
her a strand of licorice and chewing one for himself. 'Take it
from me, it'll solve all your problems.'

Unaware that she had so many, Primrose shrugged reluctantly, then went out back to speak to Herb. The Annual
Reports, published alongside those of the five other towns on
the island, were the reason for the stacks of newspapers and
lists that had covered the house's every surface when they had
moved in, and with which Primrose still had to do daily battle
in the form of those Herb refused to throw out. It was the
Annual Reports that gave importance to such mundanities as
how many books had been checked out of the library, what
percentage of rented summer mopeds had been involved in
some kind of accident, and how often the fire service had been
called out and for what cause. Of course, they also detailed
local births and deaths, the nature of the police's dealings each
season, and, most importantly for Primrose, the latest tally of

wild turkeys, whose steadily growing population had each at some point or another spent a night on the roof. It was, as she told Herb, probably the most significant job for a writer the island could offer. And when she cushioned it in such terms as that, how on earth could Herb fail to agree?

'So shall I speak to Ben and tell him you'd like to be put forward to do this year's report then?' Ben's role as year-round cab driver made him the Vineyard's most reliable means of communication. 'Apparently he can negotiate a special rate of subscription to the *Gazette*, so you can keep up to date, but really it's a matter of research and recording. It could be quite fun.'

Herb nodded. 'Speak to Ben.' And he pulled Agatha's bucket a little closer to his feet, and returned to Chapter One of his novel, a tortuous and frequently rewritten tale of a young man with a dream to wear wings. 'One day,' he promised Agatha, 'one day we will be great.' But for the moment he would settle for being published.

Just as Johnny had promised, the annual report was indeed the solution to all their problems, most immediately that of Herb and his increasingly remarked upon habit of skulking. Whereas Primrose had long traced his tendency to roam to his child-hood spent on a sheep farm, there were those who found his hanging around the lighthouse and wandering up and down the island's roads rather less ideal. Particularly now he had a child with him, and a sudden squall from behind a blackberry bush, or an unexpected face hidden in the leaves of a Beetlebung tree, could come as quite a shock if all you were expecting was the occasional crow. But with the conferred authority of the report, all this became rather more legitimate, and whereas before neighbours might have taken a detour when they saw Herb coming, these days they would stop and make chit-chat, just hoping to get a mention.

'I don't think I've ever been so popular,' Herb declared one afternoon, after a long lunch at the Home Port in Menemsha. He pulled a bag of leftovers out of his pocket, and handed it to Primrose as she maneouvred another pie out of the oven. Encouraged by Johnny, she was putting together a stall for the livestock show in West Tisbury, an attempt to restart her business after the necessary interruption of Agatha, but all was not going well.

'This pastry's falling apart,' she murmured, ignoring the paper bag of fish and clam shells Herb was still offering. 'Look at it. How on earth will I be ready for tomorrow?'

Herb shrugged. He left such domestic affairs well alone. 'Can you take Agatha?' he asked, a slight misunderstanding over the proper age to start a baby on solids resulting in a rompersuit covered in vomit and a considered need to hand over.

Primrose looked at him, shaking her head in panic and pointing once again to the pie. 'I can't possibly,' she wailed, suddenly remembering she had forgotten to add half the butter. And as she threw herself against the blank face of the fridge, Herb backed out of the room and went to find the bucket.

Agatha's bucket. Sometimes a bath, occasionally a storage place, most often somewhere to stick the baby, it had gained a set of casters and a feather cushion since Herb had first put it to use, and these days was like part of the family. When Primrose was baking and Herb needed to write, it was the bucket that took charge of Agatha, and as the months rolled by and winter scuppered back into sight, it was the one thing that remained constant. Riddled with rust and liable to leak, but constant nevertheless.

Herb's first Report was due to be delivered at the end of February, and hence in the months that preceded that he was either scrabbling away in the laundry or out roaming through fields and bars to collect his data, usually returning soaked in one way or another, and invariably a little lonelier for it. Six nights out of seven, then, it was the turkeys he sat down to supper with, Primrose's days shorter now winter was upon them and her pie business had been set aside. With Agatha learning to crawl and Johnny busy designing a range of The Wild Turkey Café merchandise with which to kick off the summer season, time for one another was in short supply.

And so Herb began to roam further, initially pandering to his long-acknowledged competitive streak by trailing after the other five report writers on the island, hiding in doorways as they counted loose dogs, dodging traffic as wandering turtles found their way into the record books, but then pursuing his interests farther afield and taking day trips to the mainland, just to check out the view. Primrose did her best to be understanding, but when one day he did not return at all, having missed the last ferry and telephoned from Woods Hole to tell her this, she decided enough was enough.

'We're a family, Herb,' she insisted, sitting him down at the kitchen table next morning and handing him a piece of pie. 'We need to behave like one.'

'And we don't?' asked Herb, genuinely surprised.

Primrose shook her head. 'You're never here any more,' she told him, twiddling her plaits nervously and hating to nag. 'And when you are you're either writing or disappearing somewhere with Agatha.' She paused, noticing Johnny outside the window, waving a T-shirt at her and pointing to the wild turkey motif. She waved him inside, then considered her point. 'I just think we need more time as a family,' she concluded, clearing Herb's empty plate and holding out her hand.

He took it. 'Sure,' he agreed, making a mental note to keep the ferry times with him to prevent this from happening again. And he untangled his fingers from hers, threw a broad grin at the ever lovely Johnny, and headed out to the deck to pick up his daughter. 'Come on, family girl,' he announced, looking back towards Primrose and making sure she heard. 'Let's me and you go find some shells to play with.' And he wheeled her bucket off the steps and down the beach to the cliffs.

Since talking to the fishermen on Menemsha docks to get their catch records, Herb had discovered a particular clam shell called an angelwing, and it was to Lobsterville beach on the other side of the lighthouse that he now wheeled Agatha, intent upon stringing a bunch together for her as a rattle, or necklace, or whatever it is that little girls of nine months liked to play with. Scrabbling around on the tide line, he picked up handfuls of the things, some still clamped together, and passed them to the waiting Agatha, propped up against the side of the tin tub. As he dug deeper however, searching for the most perfect, he did not notice the tide was coming in, and when he turned around the next time, his pockets bulging with clacking shells, Agatha was nowhere to be seen.

'Agatha,' he called, as though he expected her to answer. 'Agatha, where have you gone?'

He moved back towards the edge of the tide, feeling it soak through his sneakers, cold and threatening, and glanced up and down the beach. 'Agatha,' he howled, beginning to panic, his first, irrational thought being how he might tell Primrose he had lost her. 'Agatha. Agatha.'

Out of the corner of his eye, he saw something over by the cliffs waving, and as he turned towards it, he saw it was Agatha, or maybe it was just her hair, caught in the wind, bobbing up and down in the bucket, the currents of deeper water dragging her out of sight.

He began to run, yelling, towards the cliffs, pulling off his coat and sweater as he did, then launching himself into the biting waters, all the while his eyes fixed upon Agatha. 'Wait, wait,' he screeched, whether to Agatha or the sea or simply the horror that was happening, and as he pounded up to his chest, swimming hard against the thrashing Atlantic, he thought he would never reach her.

And then in the silence of all that crashing water, something went still, and through the spray his arms threw in all directions, he saw Agatha sit a little taller in her bucket and begin to smile. Suddenly she was waving, both hands clapping and flailing, excitedly drawing him towards her in that slapping, exposed sea, until he was at her side, fighting to keep a hold on the all too buoyant bucket, kicking for the shore.

He could not even look at his daughter as he dragged both her and bucket back on to the beach – Agatha still giggling and waving as though this were the best fun they had had in ages – and as he lifted her into his arms and held her tight against his dripping, shivering body, he was sobbing in shame.

'Agatha, Agatha, Agatha,' he murmured, pulling her hard against his face as she strained away from him. Leaning back in his arms, she reached for her bucket, as if aware that he would have happily hurled the thing into the ocean rather than wheel it home again, and as they began the slow jog home, bucket trailing a piece of seaweed in their wake, the only casualty the now sodden feather cushion, he swore never to let her inside the thing again.

Of course, days later, after Primrose was over the shock

and had let Agatha off her lap for a minute or two, she was straight back to her favourite place, where she felt safest, and no matter how many times Herb lifted her out of there and into the new walker or trolley he had bought her, she was back again as soon as he turned his head. Indeed, when she learned to walk, she even began to push it back down the beach and into the water, a couple of times making it as far as the end of the groyne before she was spotted, and eventually they gave up their efforts to dissuade her of this and simply tied several pairs of Primrose's purple tights to one of the handles and thus made sure she never got far.

Hence, it was quite a lesson Herb learnt that day with the shells, and when eventually he came to string them together they served more as a rosary for him than any kind of toy for Agatha. Counting each shell as he pushed it through his fingers, he recited his blessings and knew he had been lucky, and when Agatha was old enough to understand, he offered much the same observation to her.

But Primrose knew better. And when she tied those tights to Agatha's bucket, her fingers were trembling as she knotted feet and gussets, this being one more example of this habit she had of making do. While her husband went on day trips to get a little perspective on his life, and her daughter sailed the high seas while still too short to reach the table, she slammed pies around the oven, checked ferry timetables before laying the table, and told herself her life on the beach was perfect. And yet somewhere in the back of her romantic-fictioned mind, she saw the flaws, and knew there was only one answer.

She needed to redecorate.

Following the success of her stall at the livestock fair the previous August, Primrose had received a number of regular orders from year-rounders that kept her ticking over long past the time when they put up the storm windows and most of the island disappeared to the mainland. With a steady income, plus the occasional windfall from a particular dinner or catered event, money was no longer an issue in the household, and after buying herself two new ovens and a fridge-freezer, she decided it was time to make the house their own. Down came Wenonah's postcards, down came her lists and photographs of herself with holidaying celebrities, down came her curtains, light fittings, and even her birds. (The turkeys had never wholly broken their alliance with Wenonah, and with all her things flying into the dunes with the next gust of wind, or the last of Primrose's patience, they decided to make themselves scarce.) Primrose even took a wet cloth to Wenonah's blackboard, those recipes that mattered now firmly etched upon her mind, and as Johnny Macgregor arrived to ring the changes, paintbrush in hand, already it was a different house.

'Wow. You've been busy.'

Primrose nodded. 'Except in the laundry room. Herb's locked himself in and is refusing to come out. He claims he's quite happy with everything just as it is, but I can see he's not.

How many other men do you know spend half the week wandering around lighthouses or taking the ferry back and forth, just to have something to do? He's feeling rootless, unsettled. He needs to feel he is home.'

Johnny nodded, happy to take Primrose's word for it. 'So you want me to paint the walls?' he asked, first handing her the prototype for a Wild Turkey keyring he was working on. She smiled, handing it back again, then continued.

'I've picked out some colours which I've asked my mother to send from England. I just didn't know where to start when I saw all the charts, so I went for some I knew from London. They should arrive by the end of the week.' Since Agatha's birth, Primrose had been in contact with her parents almost weekly, usually discussing nothing more than the weather, or, as in this case, the colour of the walls, but knowing they were there was increasingly a comfort. 'Do you think you could start without the paint?' she asked, the chipped plaster and drawing-pinned walls an answer in themselves.

'Sure,' shrugged Johnny, who tended to spend most of his days at the house anyway, working or not. 'Just point me.'

Primrose led him towards the bedroom, the most dramatic of her clean-ups. Piles of postcards were stacked along the sill and floor, and as the wind lifted and fell, breezing through the open window, every so often a card lifted with it, tipping over the ledge and disappearing into the dunes. 'This room will be purple,' she announced, holding up an old pair of tights to the wall and nodding appreciatively. 'Purple like the asters on Middle Road last autumn. And then in this corner, Agatha's corner, I've chosen a rather lovely green. Kind of National Trust green, my mother would say. The whole effect will be a bit Wimbledon, but I kind of like that.'

Johnny nodded, such allusions lost upon him beyond the reference to the asters. 'You're not just going for the white again then,' he confirmed, glancing at the puckered, sun-marked walls. 'She'll really have gone, won't she?'

'Wenonah?' Primrose took his hand, squeezing it hard. 'Not in spirit. And I'm going to stick lots of things on the paintwork, just like she did.' She pulled open her bedside drawer and pointed to several hundred aluminium foil stars already traced and cut out. Closing it, she reluctantly let go his hand as she moved back to the hall to once again test the door to the laundry room. Still locked. Shrugging, she smiled gamely at Johnny. 'Beetlebung red for the sitting-room, sea blue for the cupboards in the kitchen – we can just put another coat of black on the walls – and when I manage to get Herb out of the laundry, a lovely sandy yellow, which is going to look great with all those books.'

'He'll come out eventually,' Johnny told her, with a hint of a smile. Having spent a couple of weeks in San Francisco the previous year following up an apparent sighting of his mother in Berkeley, he was wiser to Herb than any of them could have guessed. 'For now, we've got more than enough to keep me going.' He grinned at Primrose and flashed her the keyring once again. 'Then when we're done with the house, will you think about my idea of putting out a couple of tables up front? It's the obvious way to go, you know. Have I been wrong so far? Have I?'

Primrose smiled, and pointed him back towards the bedroom. And as the house was slowly transformed, Herb predictably gave up his sit-in of the laundry room and agreed that a hint of yellow could do no harm. With even Agatha's bucket coming under the brush, a lick of undercoat and a few purple handprints her concession to the new colourfulness, at least it could not be said their lives were dull.

Chapter Nine

Agatha was three years old when Herb had his first vision. They had spent the day on the beach, teasing some kitten they had found which Agatha would later insist they take home and call Miss Marple, and as evening cast its shadows across the flats, they pulled on sweaters and began the wander home. On this particular day Agatha had been persuaded to leave her bucket at home, abandoning it on the deck where Primrose would invariably be using it as a trash bin, and as they neared the house, she began to fidget and scratch in anticipation of climbing in.

'You'll have to wait for me to empty it,' Herb warned her, reading both her and Primrose's minds.

'You'll do it straight away, won't you?'

'Of course,' Herb promised.

With the house just ahead of them, Herb turned back as he always did at that time of night, glancing at his watch and waiting for the first flicker of the lighthouse. 'Watch,' he told Agatha, but she was too busy yawning and thinking of her bucket, and she wandered on ahead. Herb waited there alone, staring up at the cliffs, watching.

Then suddenly, without warning, the sky around him filled with light, and where before had been purple summer sky there was now only gold. But when he looked at the lamp, it was motionless, the timer not set to go off for another minute or so, and as he shaded his eyes with his hand, flinching from the glare, out of all that brightness appeared a figure. And suddenly the sky was raining shells, their salt-shaker colours iridescent against the motionless black sea, and as Herb moved back to call Agatha, they were landing all around him, some on his shoes, others in the cuffs of his trousers. He could not speak, his mouth wide open but the words refusing to come, and as he gazed up at the figure on the cliffs, he could do nothing more than moan. But barely was the sound out of his mouth, than the light and the figure and the shells and the smile just disappeared, as completely and as mysteriously as they had come. Until all he had left when Agatha came running back to find him, desperate that he should come immediately for her bucket was filled to the brim with peach skins, was a pocketful of clam shells and the shadow of a smile. 'I think I just saw an angel,' he told Agatha, as she dragged him across the sand to the house. 'Up on the cliffs, an angel.' But because when they turned around there was only the pulsing red-white-red of the lamp and a distant clatter of chowder pans as Jeannie closed up for the night, there was very little Agatha could do but nod.

At least, that was how Herb told it. Nodding or otherwise, Agatha was likely to see it in quite different terms, the hour and a half her father had spent talking to some musician guy on the beach while she played with the kitten more than accounting for a certain imaginativeness when it came to the walk home. And while Herb claimed it had been a matter of minutes between him seeing the vision and Agatha returning, according to his three-year-old companion it was perhaps closer to an hour. For despite the attraction of the bucket, it had been Herb who had left Agatha and not the other way around, and as she waited for him on the beach, turning slow circles and afraid to go home empty-fathered, only Miss Marple had stayed to hold her hand.

Nevertheless she stuck with the vision idea, loyalty and a three-year-old regard for such things making this infinitely preferable to the reality of her father disappearing behind some bushes with a drummer from New York. Much as did Primrose, dropping a pie on the table in front of them and taking a handful of shells as they were offered. It was in none of their interests not to, and despite the fact that Primrose was never entirely comfortable with the part in which the man made Herb moan, in time she learned to live with it.

*

Over the years, Herb's visions took him far and wide, after that first run-in on the beach angels popping up all over the place, and while each sighting took him that little bit further afield, the fact that he always came back kept them going. Not to mention the presents he invariably brought with him, guilt, self-consciousness, or simply the fact he thought they'd like them spurring on many a dip into the joint account; and as Herb returning quickly became associated with Agatha and Primrose getting, it was hardly a surprise that they were always pleased to see him. When after one particularly exaggerated pilgrimage he returned with a state-of-the-art colour television, it was a toss-up between who they welcomed through the door first, and as Primrose twiddled buttons and chased airwaves, eventually tuning into the one and only station they could get so close to the sea, she never even asked where he had been. Several hours later, *I Love Lucy* still fizzling in the background, Ed Sullivan already a permanent fourth at table, Primrose told him she loved it and swore never to switch it off. And no matter how many times Herb explained that this was a television, not some piece of jewellery whose wearing suggested constancy, its blaring out night and day soon became as much a part of their lives as the birds on the roof or the visions on the clifftops.

'I just like to know it's there,' Primrose justified. 'What's so terrible about that?'

*

Despite his various absences, however, Herb never once slacked in his work on the Report, perhaps more than ever revelling in the freedom of a remit that demanded only statistics, and made no stipulation as to what they should be. Hence, in time, his growing liberation meant he could tailor them to suit, and if his reports were a little light on the activities of the Women's Committee, one year causing ructions by overlooking altogether the efforts of three Gay Head spinsters to knit a mile-long blanket for peace, it was only because other things caught his attention instead.

'Do you know how many graphic designers sunbathed on Lobsterville last summer?' he would demand after an arduous morning of interrogations on the beach. 'And how many of those graphic designers do you imagine are fans of Carly?' (Carly – or Carly Simon – was a summer kid made good, and with a house in the area, she was an important statistic for the ever starry Herb.)

Primrose shrugged. 'And how many of those graphic designers with a love of Carly Simon ate one of my pies in the last week?' she demanded, considering it was time she got a little free publicity.

'I didn't think to ask,' he told her, flicking through his notebook for another statistic he could impress her with. A bang on the door behind him made him turn around, and as Agatha wandered in, dragging a string of saucepans behind her which she had been using as a drum kit – it was the survival of the noisiest, those typewritered televisioned days – he held up his arms to her and grinned. 'Special girl,' he declared, as she fell against his chest, hugging hard. 'Where've you been all day?'

'Here,' she told him, pointing out front where she had spent the morning dressing up with a depressed Miss Marple, and the afternoon throwing tea parties in the bucket for her imaginary friends. 'I was waiting for you to get home.'

'Well, I'm here now,' he told her, sitting her on one of his legs and studying her carefully. 'Did you get even more beautiful, special girl?' he asked her, tucking her hair behind her ear and glancing towards Primrose who was busy making a pastry turkey to sit on top of her pie. 'Is it possible she could have?' he asked Primrose, who, having missed the rest of what he said, simply nodded in agreement.

And as Agatha sat back, basking in these moments of attentive glory, being special seemed the only thing to be.

And this was a Martha's Vineyard childhood. A childhood when being five seemed older than the hills, and being wise was second nature. While Herb preached local statistics and Primrose the art of baking blind, Agatha took the advice of both and paddled ever on. Her only cares these first few years were spotting potential angels before Herb did, learning how to destalk blueberries without squirting her T-shirt, and charting whichever direction the fish were swimming, for this could radically affect one's drift. Anything more was to miss the point. Agatha never imagined that being five was a temporary state, or that some day all this might be lost. She could not imagine a future in which Herb was not carrying a copy of *Sans Souci* or *Dial M for Murder*, and an equally mysterious excuse for where he had been. No, for the moment she was five years old, sunkissed and freckled, and the only thing that set apart this particular three-foot-nothing bundle of limbs from any other child of that height or age was the long-held belief that she was special, and the refusal to appear as anything less.

'Do you know who I am?' she would demand of passers-by, standing on her upturned bucket and surveying her audience on the beach.

And while they shook their heads, mumbled something about her mother being the pie lady, and returned to their tans, Agatha would be left seething and unrecognised, wondering how this could be.

When she repeated all this to Herb, insisting he go and search them out and tell them just exactly how special and important she really was, he would just smile.

'Since when did you need public approval to be special?' he asked her, leading her down the steps and proceeding to share with her that day's findings. 'It's what you know that matters,' he told her. 'And don't you ever forget that. It's the dull ones who get the applause. Be different, be special.' He paused, wrapping his arm around her bony shoulders and squeezing tight. 'Be my Agatha.'

Being Agatha, then, was something of a mystery, which is exactly what one would hope from a child named after a crime writer and parents without a clue. While other children romped through kindergarten, wailed in and out of au pairs, and pestered the living daylights out of the family pet, Agatha bobbed up and down in her bucket with Miss Marple and searched the view for Herb. On an angel day when she knew she would not find him, she would make believe instead, shifting her piles of coloured crayons and lemonade bottles and imagining parents with time for such games, and it was not uncommon to find her still there at nightfall, bailing out the tub with Twinkie wrappers and marvelling that her guests had stayed so long. She was in a world of her own, and should anyone try to distract her, be it Primrose in need of an extra pair of hands, or some passing tourist rather disturbed by a child adrift, she would simply ignore them and carry on. On one particularly stubborn occasion, when the winds had lifted and the tide was threatening ever stronger, it took Primrose, Johnny and a somewhat confused representative from the Cape Fisheries Corporation to drag her back to shore, heaving on the purple tights like mice on a bell pull, and even then Agatha was paddling against them.

'I'm busy,' she hollered, up to her elbows in water, Miss Marple doing her best to stay calm. 'Can't you just let me alone a while and stop fussing? I'm different, don't you know. Special. It's fine just to let me go.'

'Inside, Agatha,' insisted Primrose, heaving her on to the beach and pushing child and cat towards the deck. 'It's time you were in bed.'

And as she did as she was told, reluctant and yet having found obedience to be the best way, she was already planning the crew for her next excursion. 'I'll be in my room,' she announced, heading for the depths of her seaweed-coloured corner. But as soon as their backs were turned, Primrose eager to get back to her television, Johnny working on the latest catalogue of merchandise he was convinced they could sell, Herb who knew where, she was out the window and back in her tub. They none of them knew better.

And then one September, when Agatha was six, winter brought the School Inspector blowing about their door, horrified to discover this absent pupil perched on the stove-top plaiting dried seaweed for a turnover, and discussing that year's surprisingly large number of abandoned bicycles. Hovering on the deck, wondering that they had ignored his reminders for so long, he demanded she be put into class the following Monday, and threatened court cases and general disrepute if they refused.

'The child needs to be educated,' he declared, opening his files and making a note against their name. 'It's a matter not only of law but of constitutional rights. Denying her a good education is tantamount to abuse.'

Herb was horrified. 'Abuse?' he demanded, slamming through the screen door and meeting this intruder face to face. 'How is this child abused? Look at her. Is she suffering? Is she troubled?' Agatha looked up, pressing her nose against the window and smiling broadly. Behind her, Primrose shook her head in shame. Herb continued undeterred. 'And for your information, she is being educated right here. Educated in the things she will need, not the fluff and nonsense you want for her. Go on, ask her. Ask her anything? Then I'll talk to you about abuse.'

The inspector rolled his eyes and moved a little closer to the window.

'Five times seven,' he demanded.

Agatha thought for a moment. 'Five times last season seven skunks got themselves caught underneath Jeannie's trailer and had to be pulled out by their tails.'

Herb chuckled, while Primrose sank to the floor. The inspector stepped closer.

'When was the Battle of Hastings?'

'Summer '74,' Agatha announced, without hesitation. 'She wanted the house and custody of their two children, he just wanted the house. They went to court back in Boston and he won both because she drank too much.' She looked at Herb for approval and he grinned appreciatively. There was no one who showed quite the same interest in his work as did Agatha.

The inspector once again took out his file and wrote at length on a clean sheet of paper, handing it to Herb with a grimace. 'Monday morning, Chilmark School. Make sure she's there.'

Herb looked at the piece of paper, then tore it down the

middle, scrunching both parts and hurling them towards the beach. Glaring at the inspector, he was about to suggest he pick up his litter and leave, when Primrose appeared at his side and took his arm.

'She'll be there,' she promised, glancing back towards the glowing Agatha. And she led Herb inside.

Herb was furious. 'How could you do that?' he demanded, shaking himself free of her grip and crossing towards Agatha. 'She's doing fine here at home with us. She's learning far more than school would ever teach her. How could you promise to change all that?'

Primrose shook her head, sitting down and clasping her hands around her rolling pin. 'She needs to go to school, Herb, don't you see?'

He frowned. 'No, I don't see,' he declared. He could not even begin to imagine his days without Agatha in them.

'She needs friends of her own age, children with the same interests. She needs to play.'

'I do play.' Thus long silent, Agatha leaned towards her mother. 'And I have plenty of friends, who all like the things I like.'

Herb nodded supportively.

Primrose dropped her head on to her hands. 'But not all friends have to be invisible,' she mumbled, thinking of the tribes of Lady Macbeths, Joan of Arcs, Little Nells and Eleanor Rigbys with which Agatha claimed to fill her days. She looked at Herb, imploring him to understand. 'This is for Agatha, we have to do this,' she insisted. 'Just this once, it has to be for her.'

Of course, almost on principle and with some encouragement from Herb, Agatha hated going to school. That was to be expected, given she was a good head taller and a lifetime more articulate than her classmates, regular kids with spellings to learn. She had no time for their playground games and tittle-tattle; she could sail to France and back and take tea with Elvis Presley by the time they had decided what to play, and as the weeks and months went on, she came to regard school in much the same terms as did Herb. A waste of her precious time.

'Why can't I stay at home today?' she insisted one morning, cross-legged on the beach in her pyjamas. 'We're hardly doing anything important, and I could help Herb with his proof-reading if you told them I was not well.'

Primrose shook her head. 'It's not up to me,' she told her. 'It's the school makes the rules.'

Agatha leaned forwards and slammed her hand against the lapping waves, deliberately trailing her bedclothes after her. 'It's not fair, you know,' she told Primrose. 'And it is up to you, because I already asked Herb and he said I could.'

Primrose frowned. 'Well, your father shouldn't have said that.' He was doing this all the time at the moment, and Primrose was tired of not being supported. She picked up the bundle of now soaking sheets, and squeezed them against her chest, the water drizzling down her front and legs and creating elastic bubbles on the dry sand. 'Please, Agatha, just go today. Tomorrow we'll talk about it again.'

'Tomorrow you'll say exactly the same.'

'I won't. Please, Agatha. It's only another week until you finish for Christmas. Do it for me.'

And because doing it for Primrose or doing it for Herb was all she had ever known, Agatha conceded and went to get dressed. Listening to Herb as he clattered away on his type-writer, collating all his work from the summer into a final draft he would then add to in the final run up to spring, she longed to poke her head inside, just to see what he was doing. But both because she knew how much he hated her reading over his shoulder, and because defying Primrose was not some-thing she had tried before, she refrained. 'I'll see you later,' she mumbled, first to one closed door, then another. And with a wave to Miss Marple she clanked out on to the deck and up the beach towards school.

Chapter Ten

Agatha never heard the battles that began with the slamming
of the screen door each morning, and as she climbed up the
cliff path and on to the road, any screeches or shrieks she
heard were invariably put down to the turkeys. But as dishes
flew in all directions, and typewriter ribbons hit the deck,
what Agatha took to be a little creative tension unstrung itself
to become yet another full scale row. It was not so much that
the two of them, Herb and Primrose, had anything in particular to rail against, but rather that with Agatha out all day at
school and Johnny gone west once more to follow up a lead
on his mother, if nothing else it was something to do. The
boom in Primrose's pie business following the filming of *Jaws*
on the island the year before had since tailed off somewhat,

and as the winter economy tightened its belts, she was happy that her life revolved a little less around pastry. Similarly, after six years of Annual Reports Herb had rather lost his enthusiasm for the minutiae of his neighbours' worlds, and with that winter's spate of increasingly rough weather, even his visions were thin on the ground. And so they bickered just to have something to do. But when the bickering turned nasty and the nastiness got personal, neither could pretend they had not seen it coming.

'Did you tell Agatha she didn't have to go to school today?' Primrose was standing in the doorway of the laundry room, watching Herb as he typed.

He nodded. 'One day wouldn't do any harm.'

'But it isn't one day. You said the same to her twice last week, and virtually every day of the week before. Every time you get bored with working, you suggest she stays home from school. It's not fair, Herb, don't you see that, it's really not fair.'

He looked up, surprised by her tone. 'Meaning what?' Standing up, he walked towards the window and looked out on to the back deck. Miss Marple was curled up on a pile of old deckchairs, safe from the clipping wind, and over by the dunes, Agatha's wet bedclothes slapped noisily on Primrose's makeshift line.

'Meaning we need to be united on this one. We need to agree about what we say to Agatha and then stick to it. You're not the only one who misses her during the days, you know, but she has to go to school. Or she'll never go anywhere.'

Herb scowled, opening the door on to the back deck and stepping outside. He hated Primrose in his work space, especially when she brought a fight with her. 'And where do you want her to go?' he asked, gazing around the house towards the Atlantic. 'Back to England? To London? Where you wish you could go too?'

'No.' Primrose leaned against the railings, flicking at the peeling paint with her thumbnail and watching it fall like snow on the deck at her feet. 'I just want her to have some choice. Like we did.'

'You think we had a choice? You think I did?' Herb was leaning hard against the wall now, his breath coming in short rattling gasps. 'Do you imagine if I had a choice I'd be here now?'

Primrose flinched, the challenge coming like a slap to her face. 'Yes.' She too was breathless, 'Yes I do.'

Herb turned around, his features washed as pale as the icy wintry sky above them. 'Well I wouldn't,' he told her slowly, watching as the tears sprung to her eyes and her chest began to heave. 'And if you had any sense at all, neither would you.'

And then something inside Primrose just seemed to snap, sending her flying at him across the deck with a fury she did not know she felt, but seconds later she was hitting him as if her life depended on it. Her hands beating around his head, her only aim was to hurt him, and as he ducked lower, grabbing at her fists but unable to hold on to them, he was helpless to defend himself.

'You bastard,' she wailed, now kicking, her bare feet jarring against his legs, his stomach, his head as he crumbled to the floor. 'How dare you do this to me, how dare you!' And when at last her fury was spent, her body drooping to the deck with much the same defencelessness as had Herb's, it was these words she kept repeating, over and over. It was almost an hour before Herb managed to pull himself to his feet, his body aching and mussel-shell blue, and another hour after that before he went back to get Primrose. By this time the deck was a haze of pelting rain, crashing about her sinking frame and running down her upturned face as she allowed him to drag her inside. Dropping her inside the door of the airing cupboard, he threw a towel over her head and one about her slopping body, and then slowly returned to the laundry room where he closed the deck door and laid down beneath his desk.

When Agatha got back from school the house was in silence, and at first she assumed they must both be out. But when she found her mother draped around the boiler, steaming damply as tears coursed down her face, she knew Herb could not be far away, and within minutes she was running between the two of them, desperate to patch things up.

'Just be good to one another, can't you?' she pleaded, one hand on the airing-cupboard door as she peered into the laundry room and under Herb's desk. 'It doesn't need to be like this, don't you see? It doesn't have to hurt.'

Yet it did. Even after the clothes had dried and the bruises healed, the memory of Primrose's rage stayed with them and the tears refused to dry. When, a week later, Agatha got home from school to discover her mother back in the airing cupboard, only this time having packed a bag first, whether or not it hurt seemed the least of their worries.

'I think she needs help,' she told Herb as he cradled his final draft of the report on his lap, a late statistic of domestic abuse just making the deadline, 'I think maybe she needs to go away.'

Herb shrugged and stood up. 'Fancy seeing a film?' he asked, picking up that week's *Gazette* and flicking through to see what was on. 'It's an Agatha Christie,' he told her, this clearly the best news he had had all week. 'A Miss Marple at that. *Sleeping Murder*. You want to see it?'

Agatha nodded reluctantly, one eye to the airing cupboard. 'Do you think we should?'

But because 'shoulds' had gone out of the window about the time Primrose threw her first punch, she shrugged and went to fetch her coat. With a knock on the cupboard door and a promise to bring back some popcorn, they were away, leaving the television blaring in the kitchen, and Primrose with her head wrapped around the heating pipes. It was a matter of carrying on.

Primrose waited until their footsteps were no longer audible, their voices but a trail of syllables on the wind, then carefully opened the door. From where she sat she could just see through to the kitchen, the corner of the television cutting a slice out of the room and as she listened the new contestant on *Jeopardy* was just being introduced. Primrose loved *Jeopardy*. Pulling herself to her feet, she rubbed a towel across her still tear-stained face, and stepped out of the airing cupboard, moving tentatively towards the kitchen. Holding on to the fridge, she gazed at the television, fitting questions to answers, then looked around for something to eat. The fridge was empty save for a half-drunk carton of milk and a packet of cigarettes belonging to Ben which she had intended to keep fresh until she saw him again. Taking out the cigarettes, she considered the packet, then spun a half-circle and flicked on the gas hob. The cigarette puckered between her lips, she leaned forward and held it in the flame, inhaling loudly and just catching her plaits as they swung past on either side. The kitchen filled with the smell of burnt hair, but she didn't care. Then, her head spinning comfortingly, she sank down on to her thighs, folding in on herself like a collapsed picnic table, and tucked her head between her knees, taking a drag every few seconds from the cigarette held underneath her leg.

And then Primrose remembered she was hungry. On the floor opposite her the vegetable rack heaved with the ageing remains of the pie ingredients, their once bright, distinguishable colours now merging into a single shade of brown, and as she reached to take a tomato, it burst in her hand, spilling dark red juice and sticky seeds across her front. Primrose shook her head, hating such waste, and pulled the rack towards her, steering it across the floor and under the table, then following after with a knife and saucepan. Pulling the chair behind, she was safe.

The television still blaring above her, she set about the mounds of fading fruit and vegetables, her knife undressing each with a care more befitting of a lover, her face set with concentration. Catching their skins in the lap of her dress, she worked her way through the rack, placing each carrot, potato, squash, banana, blueberry in the pan beside her, until there was only a rotten sweet potato and a half-eaten apple left, neither of which she had a taste for.

Edging backwards out from under the table, she lifted the pan on to the still burning ring, and balanced the lid on top. Then she propped open the kitchen door, inched the volume on the television up the last few notches Herb had shrunk from, and wandered out on to the deck, the pan sizzling and hissing behind her, the room thick with the bruised smell of skins and peel. There she dropped on to a chair, sweeping at her sweating brow with one of the paper napkins Johnny had stencilled with their logo, and fell fast asleep.

When Herb and Agatha got back, the house was thick with smoke from something Primrose had left cooking on the stove but which long before had burnt dry, and there were five volunteer firemen aiming hoses at the back deck, alerted by someone up on the cliffs who was worried it would spread to the dunes. Primrose was leaning against the front railing, still clutching the paper napkin, her skirt dropping curls of vegetable peel with every gust of wind, her legs and arms mushed with sweet, rotting flesh, and when Herb came to stand behind her she simply dropped back on to him, grateful for the support. Neither spoke. And as the television echoed across the beach, scorched but still deafening, he rested his hands upon her shoulders, and, like two halves of the same shell, pulled her tight against him as she began to shake.

It was Johnny who called the clinic and booked Primrose in, depressions and minor breakdowns a common occurrence on an island whose population, and hence economy, more than halved come Labor Day, and as he drove her to the ferry, he promised her she was not the first. When the car from the clinic met her at the other side, it offered similar wisdoms, the driver going to great lengths to catalogue his previous pick-ups from the island and determined to find one they both knew.

'Really, I don't know very many locals,' Primrose insisted. 'Mostly I get to meet the tourists, and I'm sure they don't suffer depressions because they always get to go home.' She turned to the window and looked out, watching the sea fade to houses and shopping malls, finding relief in its absence. 'I hate this place,' she murmured, staring at her hands and sighing as once again the tears began to stream.

And while the driver considered this was something patients usually said once they had arrived, he kept his eye on the road and left her to it. 'Damn crazy people,' he murmured to himself, considering he should put in an expenses form for the amount of counselling he was expected to provide. And behind him on the back seat, Primrose began to vomit.

They kept her in the clinic three months, missing Christmas, New Year, and much to Johnny's horror, the first pinkletink of Spring, and by the time she made it back, subdued and a little fatter, she was not the only one to have changed. For they had decorated the house in her absence, the fire having left streaks of black smoke on every wall and surface, and free from Primrose's determined creativity, Herb had opted for the infinitely calmer option of white. Brilliant, glossy white. Much like the clinic.

Primrose stared from Herb to the walls, and remembered her promise to be strong. Walking into the hall, she ran a finger along the white blank spaces of her new life (for that is how the doctors had encouraged her to approach it) and took a deep breath. 'It looks lovely,' she told him, and only the silver stars on the bedroom ceiling which had refused to come unstuck offered any reminder of what had been. Reaching for Agatha, who until now had been trailing behind, a wad of tissues in her back pocket just in case of relapses, Primrose pulled her close and kissed her cheek.

'I missed you both so much,' she breathed, glancing at Herb over Agatha's shoulder and giving him her hand. 'Did you miss me too?'

And Herb, who had waited for her return with a desperation he would never have guessed at, nodded dolefully. 'We thought you were never coming back,' he told her. 'We thought you'd gone for good.'

That she might not have come back was a prospect that had occurred to all of them. Indeed, even Primrose's parents in London had offered their twopenneth, her mother taking the first flight she could get into Boston, then spending a week at her daughter's bedside in an attempt to convince her to come home. But Primrose was adamant.

'I'm staying, Mummy,' she told her, her fingers clasped around her mother's rings, twiddling them nervously. Primrose gazed at the beige-suited stranger her daughter could call grandma. 'Agatha is here, and I'm married to Herb. This is my home.'

'But Agatha would come with you. And strictly speaking, you're not married to Herb are you? Just living with him, the whole point of which should be that if it doesn't work out, then you're not tied. As for this being your home . . .' She looked around the room. 'The clinic is your home? Really, Primrose, you need to think very hard about your life. And you need to decide what it is you want.'

'I want what I have,' Primrose insisted, her mother's whittling reminding her of why it had been so easy to leave in the first place. 'Don't you understand that? I want what I have. Only sometimes I want it a little bit different.'

Her mother frowned, the already deep-set lines in her forehead sinking lower still, like the floor of a lock when the gates are opened. 'I just hope you're not being stubborn just for the sake of it, darling. I wouldn't want you to make these decisions for the wrong reasons.'

Primrose dropped her head back against the wall behind her and let go of her mother's rings. 'I'm happy, I told you. Why can you not accept that?'

'I can't accept it.' Her mother paused, once again studying the pale sterile walls of the clinic, then continued, 'I can't accept it because you're in here. You're packed away with,' she leaned closer, whispering, 'with a bunch of lunatics as if you're some kind of danger to yourself, and I'm supposed to believe you're okay.' She took a deep breath. 'We're worried about you, darling. We have been for some time. And despite the fact that your father was deeply hurt when you just disappeared leaving only a note, all he wants for you now is to come home.'

Primrose shook her head. 'I can't.'

'Daddy will buy your ticket, I'll even go and get Agatha, if you want. Come home, darling, come back where you belong. It really isn't worth all this heartache.'

'I can't.' The tears were streaming down Primrose's face once again, but neither mother nor daughter attempted to dry them. And as the nurse appeared to suggest Primrose should get a little rest now, they nodded their compromises, and left it at that. 'I just can't,' Primrose repeated, her mother standing in the doorway ready to leave for the airport and her flight home. 'This is where I belong.'

*

'I cut the grass after the firemen were here.' Herb was giving her the grand tour of their newly appointed home, finishing with the back deck, where so much of this had started. 'They said we were looking for trouble with it coming right up to the deck, so I borrowed Ben's mower and got rid of it. It's beginning to come up again now, but we'll just need to keep on top of it. And I put a lick of paint on these back railings. The rot set in after all that water being sprayed on them, so me and Agatha got ourselves brushes and did it a couple of weeks ago when the good weather came. We couldn't do anything for the geraniums, though,' he noted, pointing to the slush of mud and twigs that had been Primrose's one attempt at gardening. 'I think they drowned.'

Primrose twiddled with her plaits, five or six inches shorter now since the clinic hairdresser had got her scissors on the singed bits. 'Looks nice,' she told him, ignoring the sorry plants. She looked back towards the laundry room. 'How's your work?' she asked.

'Oh, so-so,' Herb dismissed, for by this time of year the reports pretty much wrote themselves.

'And your writing?' There was a fine distinction between the two. 'Have you done much?'

Herb shrugged. 'I started again when you went away. Found I wanted to write a different story all of a sudden. I'm feeling quite enthusiastic about it.'

'Can I read some?'

'Maybe. Soon. I've been burning quite a lot of the old

stuff, just to keep my head a bit clearer. A lot of pages were ruined by all the water the firemen put about, and actually it felt like some kind of release. Ditching the bits that didn't work, which was all of it, really, and starting afresh.'

Primrose nodded. 'Would you like to do that with us?' Memories of the conversation that had sparked her rather dramatic breakdown had taunted her the last three months.

Herb shook his head. 'If I did, don't you think I'd have done it by now?'

Primrose smiled hopefully, looking around for Agatha. Assuming she was on the beach, she continued. 'My mother came to see me at the clinic, did you know that?' Herb shook his head. 'She wanted me to go back to London. Said that if things were as they should be, then I wouldn't have ended up in a place like that. Was she right, Herb? Should I have gone?'

Herb rubbed at his chin, pale and nervous, then reached for Primrose, stroking her hair as his breath blew soft reassurances on her neck. 'Don't ever leave, Primrose, promise me that. This is us, here, this is our family. We wouldn't survive if you weren't around. We need you, can't you see?'

Primrose nodded. Yes, she could see. 'I'm not going anywhere, Herb. I couldn't even if I wanted to. It's like I told my mother, I belong here. I wouldn't know where else to go.'

Outside the window, the stubble of grasses in the dunes whistled in the afternoon breeze, alive with crickets and sandpipers and maybe even a pinkletink or two, for Johnny had been cultivating them in anticipation of her return. Taking

Herb's hand, Primrose held his fingers inside hers and smiled determinedly. 'Let's just keep trying,' she told him, closing her eyes and remembering the room yellow. 'Let's get back to where we were before.'

And in the hallway Agatha sighed in relief, letting go her grip on the doorframe and considering it was safe to leave them alone. Another crisis averted, it was business as usual for the girl with the bucket and imaginary friends. 'Just go with the flow,' she told President Carter as he came aboard for a little light tea. 'And help yourself to a cake.'

Chapter Eleven

Herb was a dreamer. This was not something he was particularly proud of, and nor did he have any plans to tackle the problem, but as time wore on, his tendency to live his life in the clouds seemed only to get worse. Necessarily, something changed when Primrose returned from the clinic, the house seeming somehow surer, less fraught, but when the change became a revolution and even Agatha was called to arms, it was Herb and his fantasies that saw them through.

The last few months had been eye-openers all round, and especially for Agatha – taken out of school for the period after Herb had pleaded family problems – it was a time she would look back upon for many years to come. With whole days, nights, even weeks, at their disposal, the usual routines she had

thrived upon had been thrown out in favour of a more calculated attempt at adventure, and while Herb relived his youth in
the theatre, and Agatha tried to keep up, they bought a season
ticket from the Steamship Authority and hit America.

Their first outing was to a somewhat-off-Broadway production of *The Glass Menagerie* at the Cape Playhouse in Dennis,
just north of Route 6, a rather sombre affair given Primrose
had been taken away only days before, but nevertheless one to
be repeated. A week later they ventured further afield still,
with two tickets in the front row for some new, rather
unmemorable play at Wellfleet Harbour Actor's Theatre,
which had rather less 'uuumph', as Herb put it, than the Cape
place, but was still fun. After that they tried Boston, agreeing
that, in effect, it was only a bus ride. And after that, New
York, where they even called in on Dan and Clare, to discover
Dan had been promoted to Detective Inspector, and Clare had
disappeared with some Vietnamese woman to set up a restaurant on the West Coast. Every morning on the Vineyard they
bought the papers and checked timetables, and every afternoon they set off for somewhere new, the Wild Turkey's petty
cash tin wearing a hole in Herb's pocket, but necessarily taken
along for the ride.

And it was on one such trip, this time to a workshop
production in Providence, Rhode Island, that Herb met
Michael. They were sitting in the café, waiting for the interval
bell to call them back to their seats, when a blond man in
shorts and silver sneakers glittered past their table and ordered

himself a cola at the bar. Herb could not help staring, both the fact of his loveliness and that of wearing shorts when it was three degrees under reason enough for a good hard look.

'Do you know him?' Agatha asked, leaning forward and struggling to get a better view.

Herb shook his head. 'I thought I might,' he covered, 'but I don't.'

Agatha returned to her ice-cream, but Herb was still transfixed. Up until now his angels had been rather worked upon creatures, a healthy dose of fantasy and a lot of talking doing wonders for a wasted afternoon, but this guy was different.

Agatha had gone to the bathroom when Herb seized his chance to introduce himself. Sidling up to the bar, he studied his subject in profile, then, when he turned around to see who was staring at him, looked him full in the face.

'Hi,' said Herb. 'How are you?'

'Good,' replied Michael. And just as Herb had fantasised, and exactly as many years before on a train Primrose had acted upon, he looked at this stranger and simply knew.

'Are you local?'

'Boston.'

'Martha's Vineyard.'

'Do you have a room?'

'A daughter.'

'Interesting.' The boy, Michael, with the silver sneakers, looked Herb up and down then shrugged nonchalantly. 'You're older than me, you decide,' he flirted.

And while Herb was left to guess whether the decisions expected of him were the same ones he himself hoped to make, Agatha returned from the bathroom and insisted they get back to their seats.

'So you did know him, after all,' she whispered as the lights went down.

'Kind of,' smiled Herb.

Michael joined them for a burger afterwards, watching with amusement as Herb took out the petty cash tin to pay, then holding open his back pocket as he put it away again. Agatha was fascinated by this new arrival, something in the way he moved and spoke reminding her of a movie star, an observation Michael would have taken as a huge compliment had she offered it out loud.

'What are you?' she demanded, intent upon his sneakers.

'I'm a student. Engineering. MIT.'

Agatha shifted her gaze from his feet to his bare legs, then took a slurp of her milkshake. 'How come you're wearing shorts?'

'I like shorts.'

Herb shifted uncomfortably, wondering at his chances of finding a babysitter at this time of night.

'Me too,' agreed Agatha, touching his khakied thigh. 'Here. Have some shake.' And she grinned at her father, sinking ever lower beside her, and wondered that he had so little to say.

They had missed the last train long before they left the restaurant, and when Michael offered to give them a lift back to Boston, figuring it might be better than trying to find somewhere in Providence at this time of night, Herb thought it only polite to agree. 'How is it you have a car?' Agatha wondered, their own lack of transport long having troubled her.

Michael shrugged. 'I guess I just prioritise my need to get around,' he told her, leaning across the passenger seat and handing Herb his safety belt.

'Couldn't we do that?' Agatha demanded, her shoulders sardined between the backs of their two seats.

Herb gestured for her to sit back. 'But first you could prioritise sleep,' he told her, and he pointed to the length of the back seat.

'Will you wake me up when we get there?' she asked, leaning back and closing her eyes. And as they pulled out on to Route 95, she listened to the rumble of the car beneath her and fell happily asleep.

When she awoke, the car was in darkness, and both front seats were empty. Sitting forward, she leaned across to the front window, and wiped it with the flat of her hand. Several other cars were parked over to their left, and a boarded-up trailer blocked the view behind, but apart from a dog barking furiously in the back of one of the other vehicles, the night was empty of life. Agatha rubbed her eyes and looked again. And then she heaved herself over the back of the driver's seat and opened the door.

'Herb?' She called his name loudly, but her voice was lost above the roar of traffic on the adjacent road, and she realised they were in a parking slip or layby. 'Herb?' she repeated, moving away from the car and towards the trailer, assuming they must have stopped to take a pee or get something to eat. 'Herb!' She tried one last time, cupping her hands about her mouth and bellowing as hard as she could, and as she rounded the corner of the trailer, she caught her leg on the towbar and doubled up in pain. 'Ow, ow, ow,' she murmured, rubbing at her shin and wishing Primrose was there. But just as she was about to give up and limp back to the car, whispering voices on the other side of the trailer caught her attention, and she turned around. 'Herb, is that you? Daddy? Are you there?' A man in a dark jacket appeared out of the blackness of bushes and grass which banked the trailer, but when he saw Agatha, he stopped and looked about nervously.

'Hey,' he whistled, turning to where he had just come from. 'This yours?'

A rustling and a murmuring, and Michael appeared, identifiable in that black night by the luminous bareness of his legs. He nodded, frowned, pointed towards the parked car, and mumbled that Agatha was 'with us'.

Agatha grinned, reaching out to take his hand, having decided during her dreamful sleep that she was rather in love with this new friend of her father's. 'I lost you,' she told him, looking up gladly and walking him back towards their car. 'I didn't know where you had all gone.'

He straightened the waistband of his shorts. 'You should have stayed in the car, it's not safe round here.' Glancing behind him for Herb, he then stooped to peer in the passenger window before opening the door. 'Your dad's just coming,' he told her, helping her inside.

She stopped, turning around. 'But I need to go too,' she insisted, reversing out again. 'I need to do a pee.'

'Can't you wait until we get there?'

'You didn't. Please, I'll be really quick. And Herb isn't back yet anyway.'

'Herb?'

'My daddy.'

'Of course.'

Agatha began walking back towards the trailer, but Michael caught her arm. 'This way,' he directed her, leading her towards a rather barer strip of grass nearer the road.

'But can't I . . .?'

Michael shook his head. 'That's the men's,' he told her, as he spoke Herb appearing from behind the trailer and walking towards them in what seemed to be a state of some shock. 'Come on, hurry up now.'

Agatha hurried, all the while watching as her father stopped beside Michael, then leant distractedly upon his shoulder. Because the wind was blowing in her direction, she could just catch snippets of their jilted conversation, and as she heard her father yelp 'Awake?' she waved cheerily, then yanked up her knickers and ran back.

'I woke up,' she told Herb, 'and I needed to pee.'

He nodded, his features glazed and motionless. 'Are you okay?' he asked, as she pushed past them to climb into the back seat.

'Better now,' she told him, pulling his coat over her and lying down again. 'I just didn't know where you'd both gone.'

The remainder of the journey passed in silence, Herb glaring out the window and wishing he was elsewhere, and Michael wondering what on earth he had been thinking of hooking up with a man who kept a seven-year-old in tow. Occasionally, one or the other would sigh and mutter how 'that was so stupid,' or how he 'must be mad' and at one point Agatha sat up and wondered 'what was?', 'who was?' but neither would tell.

'You can drop us at the Greyhound, if it's not out of your way,' Herb told him, when the signs for Boston promised they were getting close. 'We'll just catch the first bus in the morning.'

And Michael, who had planned to offer them his couch, nodded wearily, happy to see the back of this farce as quickly as he could.

'Is he going to come down and see us when Primrose gets back?' Agatha demanded as the car pulled away and she waved it back on to the road.

'Maybe,' shrugged Herb, pulling her under his arm and three-legging towards the waiting room.

'I liked him a lot,' Agatha revealed, squeezing her

father's hand and looking back towards where the car had been. 'I hope he does come, 'cause I think Primrose will like him too.'

Of course, months later when Primrose returned to the island, Michael had been forgotten about. Herb's resolute refusal to talk about him beyond the odd nod or grimace soon put an end to Agatha's brief love affair, and it would be years before she remembered that layby-stopping drive to Boston. Herb, on the other hand, thought of nothing else for quite some time, both horrified and exhilarated by what a moment of madness had allowed him to do, and as the reality of what he yearned for finally hit home, he bought a new typewriter ribbon and went to work.

Hence the burnings. When Primrose got back from the clinic he was up to Chapter Six, but because most of what he had chosen to write about was a lifetime away from what he knew Primrose would want to read, he spent much of the week before her return hoiking out the broiler from beneath the back deck and making ash of it. When Agatha wondered why he couldn't just put it in the bin, he told her he found burning it cathartic, and when she asked if a cathartic was what you used when you couldn't pee (*General Hospital* had a lot to answer for), he told her that was one way of looking at it.

And so there was still only a handful of pages to show for the time he had spent holed up in the laundry room, but because Primrose had come to expect nothing more, she simply offered to help him edit them when he was ready for a reader, then went to unpack her bag. She had brought a guitar back with her, a four-stringed poster-painted affair that one of the nurses had given her, and as she explained to Herb the thinking behind the idea of music therapy, she strummed a few chords and claimed she felt better already.

'You know the first song I played?' she demanded, running her hand across the multicoloured front and gesturing him to come closer.

Herb shrugged.

'Guess,' she insisted, but when he continued to look blank, never having shared Primrose's fascination with pop, she broke into song with the old 'America' number and urged him to hum along. On the beach outside their window, Agatha drew faces in the sand with a stick she had been throwing for Miss Marple (a game that Miss Marple had ignored with dignity) and wished her parents a little more up to date. While Primrose moved to an encore, and Herb wondered if four strings were necessarily more irritating than the usual five, Agatha went off in search of something more interesting to do than eavesdrop on her parents.

Hence life on the beach got back to normal, with Herb doing his thing, Primrose doing hers, and somewhere in the middle, Agatha doing what she felt like and hoping they wouldn't mind. They none of them acknowledged the tacit agreement that had been reached when Primrose chose to come back to them, the silent condonation she gave to the life she only half knew about and the dreams she would not see.

'What I don't know won't hurt me,' she told Herb, in theory referring to a letter she had received from the school's principal regarding Agatha's long absence, but clearly intended as a rule of thumb. 'You just do what you think is best, Herb. I really don't want to know.'

So Herb wrote back to the school, declaring the resolution of the 'family problems' and assuring him that Agatha would be back the following week, and as Primrose set about learning her favourite song of the year before, 'Save Your Kisses for Me', wishing that he would, the first thud of the evening landed with a squawk above their heads and it was as if she had never been away.

Chapter Twelve

Johnny Macgregor had been busy during Primrose's absence, having decided that success for the Wild Turkey Café lay beyond the bounds of Martha's Vineyard and setting up a mail order service to make his point. Primrose, who had been considering giving the whole thing up (filling pies somehow didn't do it for her the way it used to), was less than thrilled by the prospect, but given his promise to take responsibility for any extra business this generated, she eventually agreed.

'Besides, it's this place getting so quiet in winter that got you into that mess,' he told her, gesturing west with his head and pulling a face that translated as 'clinic'.

'I'm sure it contributed,' Primrose acknowledged.

'So my solution is keep busy, stay open all year round. I

mean, take a few weeks away if you like, but just call it vacation, and not three seasons off.'

Primrose nodded. 'I suppose we can give it a go,' she agreed, taking a mailing list from him. 'But if it doesn't work, or we decide it's too hard, then we close it down, agreed.'

'Agreed.' Shaking hands, Johnny grinned triumphantly, confident that mail order, however hard, however unworkable she might later argue it to be, was here to stay. You only had to look at her marriage to understand that.

That summer Primrose worked flat out, baking, filling, addressing, posting, and barely were they into June than she was exhausted and desperate for a little help. So she hired her daughter on the day school broke up, handing her a pinny and a wage slip, and as the beaches swelled still further and the demand just grew and grew, they did what Johnny had been pestering for since they started up, and set up a restaurant on the deck. Initially Herb was dead set against it, finding it hard enough to get peace to write as it was, but when Johnny – still an idol, although the following was less obvious – insisted that, actually, it would be fun, he relented and offered to serve.

'I could get to like this,' Herb announced one sundried afternoon, wiping his hands across the front of his logoed apron, and reaching for another key lime pie. ''S a great way to meet people, don't you think?'

Primrose caught his arm as he walked out the door, sprinkling icing sugar on the piece of pie he was carrying. 'Just no favours, though,' she warned, alluding to his tendency of waiving the bill in return for a little banter.

'No favours,' agreed Herb, winking at Agatha whose habits were just as bad. And he delivered the plate to the first table outside the kitchen.

'Thank you, young man,' said the dungareed gentleman with the beard and the faintly pink hands. He leaned forwards, beckoning Herb to approach, and as they met face to face above the key lime pie, he took his hand and smiled. 'It's nice to meet you, I'm Wenonah. I believe you know my son.'

It was inevitable that Wenonah would show up sooner or later, this being her home and authority never a force to scare her, but when she did so wearing overalls and a false beard, even Johnny was at a loss for words. Flying out of the kitchen, he stood staring on the deck for a good two or three minutes before he could be convinced of her identity, and only then when she let him peel back a corner of her beard to prove it was indeed a fake.

'But what are you doing here?' he demanded, lowering his voice when she shushed dramatically and glanced back towards the cliffs.

'Hiding from the police,' she told him, pressing her side-burns to make sure they were still in place. 'You won't believe the time I've had.'

'It's been fourteen years, Ma,' Johnny mumbled, suddenly remembering how mad he was at her.

'And you haven't changed a bit,' she told him. 'Still my beautiful boy.'

Primrose poked her head out of the window to see what was happening, Agatha having gabbled something about a man called Wenonah, then disappeared beneath the deck, and as she beckoned for Johnny to return, his companion smiled approvingly.

'Good to see you got yourself a good woman,' she told him. 'What's her name? Call her over. It's about time you settled yourself down.'

Johnny shook his head, 'Primrose,' he told her. 'But she's not mine. She's married to Herb, that guy over there. We're just business partners, Primrose and me. Friends.'

Wenonah pulled a face. 'She's married to that old queen? How did you let that happen? If I'd been around, I'd never have put up with that one.' She shook her head, beckoning Primrose over then pausing to stare at her pink hands.

Johnny stared too, echoing her 'if'.

'Damn cranberries,' murmured Wenonah. 'I should have known it was a crazy place to hide.'

Johnny closed his eyes in despair, then opened them to find Primrose standing there, smiling hurriedly.

'We're incredibly busy, Johnny.' She waved towards the kitchen.

'I know, I know, I'm coming.' He made to stand up, pushing back his chair then holding on to it for a little support. 'Primrose, I'd like you to meet my mother. Wenonah, this is Primrose, my friend.'

If Primrose was surprised that the man eating her pie was Johnny's mother, then she did not show it, instead remarking upon how similar they looked, and would she like a cup of tea? 'You're a honey,' replied Wenonah. 'But if you don't mind I'd rather keep moving along. Eleven states, eleven, they want me in, can you believe it? And the bastard who got me into this mess didn't even want me in one. What can you do?' She threw up her hands, pushing away the half-eaten pie and laughing.

Primrose smiled, and took one of those thrown hands in hers. 'Cranberries?' she asked, having suffered a similar problem herself last time they were in season, although it was a pie and not a bed she had been making. Wenonah nodded. 'Come into the kitchen,' Primrose said. 'Your kitchen in fact, as was. I've got some soap stuff that always works for me. And then maybe you can have a look at all we've done.'

'You're a honey,' Wenonah repeated, about to turn down the offer, then thinking better of it. 'All right,' she agreed. 'But just for a minute or two. It's the sitting ducks they shoot, you know. Got to keep moving.'

She stayed for two weeks, and then some, sitting, sleeping, eating, gossiping, even, occasionally, whipping up a couple of lemon meringue pies when they were stuck for an extra pair of hands. After some persuading, she even gave up the beard, too much glue, Primrose assured her, certain to add years to her already wind-chafed skin, and as she paraded around the house in a couple of Primrose's maternity dresses, not a shadow of stubble in sight, she felt increasingly at home.

'We kept all your things, you know,' Primrose told her, 'in a trunk beneath the house. Herb can't bear to throw anything away, so he just packed them all up. They're all there if you want to look.'

Wenonah shook her head. 'Life is all about knowing when to let go. And that junk is most definitely the past as far as this old girl is concerned.' She had a habit of talking in the third person, something Johnny put down to an ongoing struggle to live with herself. 'Burn the lot of it, if you like. There's no other use for it.'

Agatha, however, disagreed. From her hiding place behind the industrial dishwasher Primrose had installed only a week before after a series of unreliable kitchen porters, she raised her arm, following it with a head, and then, being her father's daughter, an opinion. 'You can't burn all that stuff,' she insisted. 'All those cuttings and postcards and pictures of you with Lillian Hellman and Gregory Peck and all those speckley Katharine Cornell types.' She had spent the last week since Wenonah arrived pulling out various parts of the trunk and was now a considered expert upon the subject. 'It's historical. You can't get rid of that.'

Wenonah threw her a sugary smile, then batted one of her now faded pink hands. 'You can get rid of anything, if you set your mind to it. The secret is not to get sentimental.'

Agatha smiled back, more treacle than sugar. 'I just think

you should take a look, before you just dump it. It would make a great record of the island, of your life. You could even ask Herb to write the text. He's good at stuff like that.'

Wenonah raised her eyebrows. 'I got plenty of records of my life. Most of them fitted with a mugshot and marked "Wanted". I don't need more, and when you get to my age, maybe you'll understand why.'

'Maybe. Maybe not.' If she had learnt anything from her parents it was to back an argument each way. 'Will you at least look at a couple of pictures?'

For want of some peace, Wenonah relented, and for the next five hours Agatha trawled with her through the stacks of photographs and postcards which had once filled the house. Writing the names and places on the back of each, she filed them in a tower of butter cartons her mother had given her for just this purpose, and tucked them beneath her bed, claiming it was drier up here than under the deck.

'What is it that you find so interesting in all this?' Wenonah demanded. She gazed at the child with her scouring-pad hair and too-small jeans with the patches on the knees from listening at too many keyholes. 'Other than the fact you're a nosey-poke?'

Agatha shrugged, not in the least put out by this characterisation. 'Just that,' she admitted, writing the year and both their names on the top of the box. 'And it's interesting, isn't it.'

'It's stuff, that's all. Just stuff.'

Nevertheless, Wenonah's life was catalogued and filed away for future reference, Agatha planning a book, or at the very least, an essay, on this woman who thought her mother was sweet and her father some kind of royalty.

'Don't you think she's amazing?' Agatha asked her mother as they watched Wenonah feeding part of her beard to the turkeys.

'I suppose she is,' agreed Primrose.

'I mean, kind of special?'

'I don't know. I suppose she is.'

And as the sun set above a house of exiles, streaking the sky a faded pink not dissimilar to Wenonah's hands, Agatha imagined them to be two of a kind, herself and Johnny's mother, and went out back to feed the remainder of the beard to the cat.

That Wenonah and Herb did not get on was obvious from the very start. Even without Agatha's retelling of the 'old queen' remark – she had assumed it was a compliment, Primrose's love of the British monarchy allowing nothing less – they were on shifting ground, and when Herb thought it would be amusing to invite the Chief of Police to the café for lunch, resulting in Wenonah quivering inside the dishwasher for the entirety of the shift, there seemed very little left to add. And yet they managed. When Herb went off on one of his regular statistic-chasing afternoons, she wasted no time in trashing him to her son and prospective daughter-in-law. (She had high hopes for Primrose once she helped her to her senses.) And when that didn't work, Primrose meeting all her charges with an 'I know, but it's the way he is, and the way he was when I fell in love with him, so what can I say?', she decided upon a more calculated attack, never one to walk away from a good fight.

'Why don't you just accept I've won?' Herb demanded, his face creased in amusement as he watched her climb, damp and wrinkled, from the dripping tank of the dishwasher. 'You should be grateful I just stuck to the details of the Annual Report and didn't ask him to wash a few plates.'

Wenonah squeezed the foaming detergent from her straggling grey hair and hissed venomously.

'You'll wish you had by the time I'm finished with you,' she promised.

But Herb, who, in his innocence saw this as just a bit of fun, mistook the threat for a challenge, and promptly made dates with the Chief's deputy and his wife for the following day. 'Nothing like a bit of good old teasing between friends,' he remarked to Primrose later that night, after that first day, with the beard and the dungarees, finding it all a bit of a joke. 'She can see the funny side.'

'And you're sure she does?'

'Course. Johnny said she's always been up for a bit of a scam. She's just getting a bit back of what she gives. Maybe she's met her match.'

But Wenonah had met her match long before Herb, and on several occasions too, and if any of the said 'matches' were still around to talk about the experience, regrettably they did not talk to Herb. Hence he kept up his quibbling and bantering and games, leaving flashing blue lights outside her window at night, making phone calls in deep voices and pretending it was a raid, to the point that just Primrose watching *Starsky and Hutch* had Wenonah flying into a rage. But when she warned him she did not find it funny, and even Johnny confirmed that getting jokes was not her thing, he did not listen. Like most things in his life, Herb thought he had it under control.

It was a Friday when Wenonah decided that revenge was imminent, something to do with the position of the moon and the fact she was getting itchy feet rather rushing her plans, and as she watched Herb head off for a day on the mainland, she checked her new supplies of facial hair and braces and quickly packed a bag. Then she let herself into the laundry room, locking the door behind her and removing the key, and slowly, methodically, beginning at the bookshelves, began to destroy every last thing that belonged to Herb. She tore the last page out of each of his Agatha Christies, the first out of his Annual Reports (the one with his name on, no less), poured cold coffee into the mechanics of his electric typewriter, and tore his face from his own growing collection of celebrity photographs. She emptied his drawers, throwing the contents in all directions, then cleared the surface of his desk in much the same way, and when she was done tearing and pouring, and emptying and clearing, she bundled everything she had found into a large flour sack she had brought with her for the purpose, and dropped it on to the deck outside. Then, just as she had watched Herb himself do almost every afternoon since she had arrived, she dragged the broiler out from underneath the steps, filled it with the contents of the bag, and added a match. Flames licking at the sides, she wheeled it towards the steps, walked around to the front of the house where she had dropped her bag, and left. When Johnny and Primrose emerged from their morning baking session in the kitchen to discover the back deck was on fire, they called 911, said goodbye once again to the geraniums, and only much later realised Wenonah had gone too. But by then it was too late.

'Probably best this way,' Johnny philosophised, a catch in his voice. 'She's very unpredictable, you know. I never really trust what she's going to do next.'

'Herb will miss her though,' Primrose noted. 'I haven't seen him so jolly in years. I think he enjoyed the challenge.'

'I still think it's best,' repeated Johnny.

'Well, you know your mother.'

Johnny stared at her, then at the still smoking deck. 'I haven't got a clue,' he told her. 'Not a clue.'

Nor did Herb. When he returned around midnight to find the door to the laundry room locked and the steps around the back charred and soaking, it was less curiosity, more sheer panic that sent him haring into Primrose, shaking her from her sleep and demanding to know what had gone on. When she told him there had been a small fire, a few things from his room, another tick for the Fire Service Call Outs in his report, he was hyperventilating before she could even finish her sentence.

'My few things?' he demanded. 'From my room?'

Primrose sat up slowly, shushing, 'You'll wake Agatha.'

'But how, how can there be a fire with things from my room? Who was in there? Who did this?'

'I don't know. We just came out and saw it, there was nobody else about. I thought maybe it was you, that you'd left the broiler out and forgotten about it. But when I saw what had happened to the laundry room, I knew it couldn't have been.'

'What had happened to the laundry room.' Herb repeated the words with what Primrose took to be resignation, but which would later prove to be despair, then slowly backed out of the room and stumbled outside on to the deck. Falling down the steps, he made his way around the back of the house and through the door into his room. And with his arms crossed over the top of his head, his body hanging broken beneath, he stared at the last ten years of his life torn and scattered on the floor.

He did not sleep that night, just crouched on the front steps as the beam from the lighthouse swept back and forth above him, and when Primrose got up around five, he was as grey and vague as the dawn that surrounded him.

'Have you been here all night?' she asked him. 'Just sitting?'

'Everything's gone,' he told her. 'Everything I've ever cared about.'

'Not everything, Herb. We're still here.'

'My books, my reports, ruined. And my pages just a pile of dust.'

'I'm sorry.' She shook her head. 'Were they ones you wouldn't have burnt?'

He nodded, missing the irony. 'All gone,' he murmured, 'I just can't believe it.'

Primrose sat down beside him, wrapping her arm about his shoulder and leaning into him as the wind slid off the ocean and blew the last few ashes in circles about their feet. She stayed with him for two hours, the two of them just sitting, silently, gazing out to sea like two old gulls waiting for an air stream, and it was only when Johnny arrived, clutching a batch of orders for that day, that she moved away.

'Shall I help you tidy up later?' she offered, as she backed towards the kitchen.

Herb shook his head woefully. 'I can manage.'

Somebody else did not sleep that night. Agatha. Lying in bed she went over and over the contents of the twelve or thirteen pages she had rescued from the broiler after watching Wenonah's attack on her father's room, gradually making sense of what she had found there. Somewhat charred and in various places too black to read, at first she had assumed the work to be fiction, along the lines of the Agatha Christies he was so fond of reading to her, but when she found her name there, tucked inside a car on Highway 95, the reality of the story hit home. One badly written story about one night with one man with one intention, and Agatha's world changed. As she sat there, the still hot pages burning against her bare legs, she closed her eyes and felt her childhood in this idyllic beach hideaway slip away for ever. And when she opened them again she was lost.

She never told anyone about the pages, just folded them in quarters and stuck them in Wenonah's files beneath her bed, and as she lay awake listening to her father's desperate questions and her mother's shushing, she knew she never would. Just as they had done before, she would keep the secret of their disjointed lives with all the diligence and quiet acceptance their example had taught her. It wasn't hers to break.

Chapter Thirteen

But Agatha was angry. In the pure, unadulterated way of an eleven-year-old. She didn't throw things, or make scenes. She did not even attempt some kind of confrontation, preferring that this should remain her discovery, her big deal, and as the days passed following Wenonah's disappearance and Herb's decline, nobody even noticed the change. And yet it was there. The anger, the disappointment, the gently fizzling desire to leave all this behind and find something new to believe in. It was there.

Of course, when they did catch glimpses, they just put it down to Agatha growing up. (Which, in a way, was what it was.) When she declared one afternoon soon after that she needed her own room, somewhere to call her own where she could keep her private things, Primrose for one was amazed she had waited this long.

'I know, I know,' she told Agatha. 'You're much too big to be sleeping in ours. I've just always rather liked you being there, but I understand you need some space of your own.' She thought for a moment. 'Maybe we can divide the sitting-room. Put up a partition and move your bed into there. We never really use it anyway, and that was where Johnny always slept when he was living here before.'

Agatha shrugged. 'Wherever.'

'Or there's the attic, I suppose. It's just full of boxes and junk. It might be quite nice having all that space to yourself, even if you will have to stoop a bit.'

Agatha shrugged a second time. 'Yeah,' she mumbled, 'I think I'd like the attic.' The thought of having a whole floor to herself, however short in height, rather appealed.

'Then that's what we'll do.' Primrose stuck her head inside Herb's laundry room to inform him of the news, but then changed her mind. 'I'll tell him later,' she smiled, hoping Agatha had not recognised the sobbing creature beneath the desk as her father. 'Come on, let's have a word with Johnny and see if he can help us move everything around.' And she led Agatha into the kitchen where they planned step-ladders and light fittings, and perhaps even a chute for the cat.

After that first demand was so easily met, the rest followed with speed. She did not want to work in the café any more: not a problem, they would get a student. She was bored with her bucket, could she have a bicycle: fine, they were thinking of buying her one for Christmas anyway. She hated school and wanted to get a job in The Bunch of Grapes Bookstore instead: stick it out a bit longer, there would always be books to sell.

'She's just feeling her age,' Primrose whispered to Johnny as they watched Agatha strut off the deck and along the beach, toenails glittering menacingly with the silver polish Primrose had told her looked cheap but she had used anyway. 'She'll grow out of it.'

And similarly would she grow out of the drainpipe jeans and fishing net T-shirts she refused ever to take off, or the earrings and lip gloss that turning twelve had made obligatory. While the rest of the world reeled as Israel invaded Lebanon, Grace Kelly was killed in a car crash, Britain went to war over the Falklands and Princess Diana gave birth to a king, Agatha spun circles of her own and decided she was bored.

'I hate it here,' she told her parents one sunny, sea-soaked day, as the waves curled softly over the buckets full of angel-wing shells she had dumped on the beach that morning. 'Nothing ever happens. Why can't we move?'

'Move? You can't really mean that? Where would you go?' Herb, who had spent his life swapping places, found the idea preposterous.

'Anywhere. Anywhere but here.'

'But this is where we live. This is where you were born.

This is our home.' Primrose always made lists when stuck for answers.

'But it doesn't have to be. This was where Wenonah lived, but she still left.'

Herb scowled irritably. 'Don't even say that woman's name. I hardly think she is a role model.'

But a role model was exactly what she had become, something about the determination of this wanted woman dressed as a man inspiring Agatha towards a similar end, and as she experimented with moustaches made from wads of cotton wool, and stole a couple of pairs of Herb's jeans and adjusted them to fit, it was only a matter of time before she followed her. In the light of her father's betrayal, her mother's collusion, and the general apathy of Johnny and the cat, the woman with the police record and hands stained with cranberry seemed the best bet that Agatha had.

It was the summer of her thirteenth birthday when Agatha decided to jump ship – somewhat literally, given that she was standing on the deck of Johnny's new boat at the time. The growing popularity of the island as a target for day-trippers, largely due to the increasing numbers of celebrities who had bought houses there, had encouraged the ever-enterprising boatman-restaurateur to extend his interests into the realm of whale-watching. Years before the Vineyard had got rich by killing such creatures, but a few still made stops there on their seasonal 4,000-mile trips between feeding grounds, and as one of the first to catch on to this, Johnny had invested hard. Trading in his dinghy for a glass-bottomed boat three times the size, he put up posters in the café, found a couple of sous chefs to take his place in the kitchen, and set sail on the *Primrose Belle* with hopes almost as high as his insurance payments.

Agatha, bored for something to do, joined him on the maiden voyage.

'So what happens if you crash?' She peered through the panes of glass beneath her feet, watching sand and seaweed scuttle past.

'It's reinforced,' Herb panted, thigh deep in water as he pushed them across the lapping waves.

'I told you we should have left earlier. Primrose can manage, you know. If you hadn't been fussing so much we wouldn't have missed the tide.'

Johnny ignored her wisdoms, gave one last shove, and hauled himself over the side, shaking his legs, then quickly towelling both himself and the deck. 'This is great, isn't it?' he demanded, looking back towards the shore where Primrose waved excitedly. He had wanted her to join them on her namesake, but she had felt both of them disappearing for the day would be too much. 'Wave to your mother,' he urged, glancing at Agatha, but Agatha was looking the other way.

'So do you think we'll see whales today?'

'I dunno. Maybe. A guy I know in Provincetown reckoned there's a mother and calf hanging about by the Bank, but whether they'll still be there today, who knows?' He shrugged. 'It's fun just like this, though, don't you think?'

'If you like this kind of thing.' She reached in her pocket and pulled out a bottle of red nail varnish and began elaborately painting her toes, back braced against the side of the boat, brush held high as she admired her handiwork.

'Agatha, honey, please.' Johnny gestured towards the glass floor. 'Come on.'

She stared at him for a moment, considering her retorts, then, rather unexpectedly, stuck the brush back in the bottle and returned it to her pocket.

'Have you heard from Wenonah?' she asked, gazing towards the horizon.

'Don't mention that name. You don't know how much trouble that woman has caused me.' He glanced back towards the beach, now just a thin sliver of gold, and shook his head. 'I could have lost my job and my best friend.' He hesitated, correcting himself. 'My best friends. If Herb had been less understanding, she could have ruined everything, not to mention been charged for arson too, whenever they catch up with her.'

Agatha raised an eyebrow. 'That's a nice way to talk about your own mother. And you lot go on at me . . .' She was twiddling with the leather edge of one of the bench cushions, drawing faint lines with her thumb nail.

Johnny ignored her. 'She's bad news, that's all. As far as I'm concerned, there's nothing more I want to do with her.'

Agatha stood up, crossed the deck to the other side, and

looked over. 'How deep do you reckon it is here?' she wondered, dragging her hand across the water's racing surface.

'Too deep to stand up.'

'So she hasn't written to you since she left?'

Johnny sighed. 'What is it with you? I thought I said I
didn't want to talk about her.'

'No you didn't. You said you didn't want anything to do
with her, not that I couldn't ask innocent questions.'

Johnny rubbed his hand across his forehead and adjusted
his sunglasses. How did a thirteen-year-old girl get to be so
persistent? He pulled back on the throttle, and turned them
through Nantucket Sound and north towards Monomoy island,
just below the Cape. The next few minutes passing in silence,
they were broken by Agatha.

'Have you then?' she demanded.

'Yes I have.'

'So where is she?'

'Agatha, what is this?'

'I'm just interested. After all, she's almost family.'

Touched by this last, and aware of how many more hours
he was stuck with the child, he grinned and raised his eyebrows. 'You can have her then. But you'll have to go to Philly
to get her.'

'Philadelphia?'

He nodded. 'I got a postcard from a hotel there where I
guess she's staying. Quite a shock, when you consider that the
last time she disappeared I didn't hear from her until she

showed up fourteen years later. Obviously she's getting better with age.'

'Which hotel?'

'I don't remember.'

'Try.'

'What's the big deal?'

'I'm interested, that's allowed, isn't it?'

'Agatha, you've spent a lifetime being interested. You're lucky it's never got you into big trouble, do you know that?'

She rolled her eyes and looked away. 'Did you at least keep the postcard?'

'Somewhere. I think I probably showed it to your mother.'

'So it's at the house?'

He shrugged. 'What do you reckon, humpbacks or pilots? The guy I spoke to reckoned the mother and calf he saw were whites, but I said not in these waters.'

'Humpbacks,' Agatha murmured, sliding off the bench and across the deck, then rolling on to her stomach and staring at the black depths beneath. Her short dark hair stood in spikes, waving in the rushing wind like some stranded sea anemone caught in a current, and for a moment Johnny wanted to reach out and touch it. But then she jumped up and the moment was lost.

'Can't this thing go any faster?' she demanded, leaning on the shelf of front deck and screwing up her eyes against the sun.

Johnny looked at her sidelong. 'It doesn't need to.'

'Yes it does.' Agatha leaned towards him, her eyes wide and challenging. 'I want it to.'

She watched him think for a moment, weighing up the contest, and she smiled at his transparency. 'Go on, Johnny. Let's see what this thing's made of.'

Suddenly the boat was lurching forward, faster and faster, Agatha blown backwards with the force of it, and as she struggled to stay upright she clasped the back of Johnny's T-shirt and held tight. 'More, more,' she screamed, laughing hysterically, her fingers knotting inside his T-shirt, 'faster.'

And the wind was howling and the sea was crashing and Johnny was a hero and Agatha was soaked. When they saw another boat in the distance, they steered in the opposite direction, and when land rose up to their left, grey and lifeless like the plastic landscapes that come with toy trains, they put it on their right and headed back the way they came. And all the while Agatha was shrieking, frightened and thrilled by what she had provoked, until they were back into Nantucket Sound with the ferry just ahead of them, and suddenly the engine cut.

'You stopped?' Agatha fell to one side, dropping on to her knees and gasping exhaustedly.

'Yes.' Johnny continued to look straight ahead.

'Why? That was the most fun I've had just about ever.'

'It was stupid.' He turned around, his face empty, and looked at the flooding deck. Over in the corner, by the icebox Primrose had packed for them, a silvery grey fish flapped in the inch or so of water they had taken on board, and he stooped to pick it up, throwing it back. 'Let's go home,' he said, starting up the engine and easing forward, cutting across the wake of the just-passed ferry.

Agatha made no response, only stared at her hands and a hairline crack in the deck she was sure hadn't been there before. And as they pulled around the Sound and back into the expanse of Atlantic they called their own, the only sound was the kracking of gulls above their heads, and the soft, sweet slur of the ocean.

'I'm sorry we didn't get to see any whales,' Johnny mumbled as they neared the cliffs where he moored.

'I don't care.' And indeed, whales were the last thing on her mind when she jumped off the deck and into the waist-high water he had offered to carry her through. While Johnny messed with anchors and wept over cracks in his deck, she splashed towards the beach and made straight for the kitchen where Primrose was up to her elbows in flour and attempting to negotiate with a surly washer-up. (Ever since Wenonah had taken refuge inside the dishwasher, it had never got beyond the initial rinse cycle.) She looked up as Agatha entered.

'There's a postcard,' Agatha demanded. 'Johnny said he left it here. Have you seen it?'

Primrose pointed to the back of the kitchen where she kept all the accounts and business papers. 'Everything's back there. What does he want it for?' They tended not to get too many postcards, and so Wenonah's had stood out.

Agatha shrugged, dropping stacks of paper on to the floor in her haste. Primrose began to dust off her arms in order to prevent her wrecking her impeccably organised filing system completely. 'Wait a minute, darling,' she urged, 'let me find it for you.'

But Agatha already had it, holding it above her head and waving it excitedly. 'Don't worry,' she told her, 'I'll go give it to him now.'

The screen door slammed in a small flurry of flour and sand, and Agatha was gone, pausing only to grab the petty cash tin from the hidden drawer in Table 5 – a travelling tip she had picked up from Herb – then sprinting along the beach just as Johnny was wading on to it. With a cursory wave of her hand, the postcard tucked safely in the back of her jeans, she kept running, hurdling the rafts of horizontal bodies as they lay burning in the midday sun, until she reached the cliff path. Here she had to wait a minute or two, the gradual erosion of the last couple of years making it too narrow to take two bodies at once. Standing at the bottom, tapping her feet as two overweight ladies in pleated tennis skirts and straw hats huffed and puffed their way down, she glanced behind her at the bottom of the cliffs, cordoned off now to stop people bathing in the thick red clay and hence speeding still further the gradual decline of the rockface. 'Take your time, won't you,' she murmured, betting herself they were heading for the café. They looked like pastry types.

She never found out. For barely had the first open-toed
Dr Scholl sandal reached the beach, than she was around them
and sprinting towards the top, digging her sneakers hard into
the cracked path, her elbows shooting back and forth like pis-
tons. Jeannie waved when she saw her fly over the top,
bursting out of the summer's overgrowth of grasses and dusty
miller like some wild animal heading for its lair, but Agatha ran
straight past, heading for the tour buses which parked down by
the road.

Joining a queue for the one that looked most imminent,
she slipped up the stairs alongside another tennis-skirted
matron and headed straight for the back of the coach. Tucking
herself deep into the corner, she stared resolutely out the
window until the remainder of the passengers had boarded,
then sighed in relief as they made the slow, trundling drive
down-island towards the ferry. As the rest of the bus piled off
for an afternoon's shopping and a bite of lunch at Primrose's
main rival on the island, the Black Dog Bakery – a snappy
little operation that years later would outstrip her when the
President gave his girlfriend a gift in one of their tote bags –
Agatha headed for the docks. Here she bought herself a one-
way ticket to Woods Hole, flinging herself on to the ramp of
the *Islander* just as the chains began to roll, and as the ferry
pulled into the Sound, she was shaking. Taking the postcard out
of her pocket, she held it between pinched fingers and stared
from the anonymous-looking Holiday Inn on the front to the
inscription on the other side. *Good to see you, looking well, Ma.*

And then, underneath, *xxxxx to Primrose. She should ditch the queen.* Agatha smiled to herself.

'Wenonah,' she murmured, over and over, as if it were some kind of mantra that would save her. She was on her way.

She took a bus from Woods Hole to Boston, all those theatre excursions when Primrose was in the clinic setting her up nicely for this particular journey; and such was the confidence with which she bounded on to coaches, off again to change for New York, then on to Philadelphia, that no one questioned what a thirteen-year-old girl was doing riding across states on her own, much less with only a petty cash box to hold on to. There was a vague upset at New York's Port Authority when she discovered she was two dollars short for the final leg, Herb having been dipping in and out of the petty cash himself recently, but such was the look of sheer panic which seized her every feature, the usually unforgiving ticket man waved her through without another word. As she settled herself into the grubby, still-warm seat that would take her to Philadelphia, she figured luck was on her side that night. This, like so many other journeys that had led to this place, was obviously meant to be.

When she arrived at the Greyhound station in Philadelphia, it was gone ten, a glaring, barefaced clock on the wall in the waiting room seeming all the more smug for the fact it was dark, she was in a city she did not know, and the only rattle in the petty cash tin was that of her mother's paste earrings, which she left there for safe-keeping. Floundering for a moment, she wavered on the pavement outside the bus station, watching the headlamps of those better organised than she and wondering as to her next move. And then she remembered that she had got this far on not much more than a whim, so why should she think too hard about the rest of it?

Stepping into the merry-go-round traffic of motorbikes and cars, she raised her hand to hail a taxi, and stepped back as it pulled into the kerb.

'The Holiday Inn,' she announced, slamming the door behind her and leaning back.

The driver, a young man with slick black skin and an ear-ring, glanced at her in the mirror, then pulled off, using his hand through the open window to wave himself into line, every so often slamming his hand on the horn when he didn't get his way. Agatha sat motionless on the back seat, wishing only to arrive and hoping that by the time she did so she would have thought of a plan.

'Where you from?' The driver turned around in his seat as they waited at the lights, flicking his chin at her as if to clar-ify it was Agatha he was addressing.

'Massachusetts,' Agatha told him, going for the broader picture.

He whistled. 'You on your own?'

'I'm meeting a friend. At the Holiday Inn.'

'Hope he's good to you, making you come all this way on your own.'

'He's a she. And yes, she is.' Agatha wound down her window, feeling the night air rush at her face and dropping her head for a moment. She was tired. 'I'm going to have to get you to wait a moment when we get there, while I run in and get some money from my friend. I kind of overspent.'

He turned around and studied her briefly, then turned back again. 'Sure,' he agreed. 'I guess I can trust you, right?'

Agatha nodded. 'Is it far?' she wondered, the cold air on her face beginning to lose its effectiveness.

'Right at the next lights. Soon be in bed.'

And right at the next lights it was. As they pulled up outside one of the many shoeboxed, soulless hotels the city was spattered with, Agatha peered up at the chessboard of dark and lit windows, and hoped Wenonah's would be one of the latter. 'Can you wait?' she checked, opening the door and climbing out.

'Sure thing.' Climbing out with her, he followed her towards the sliding doors and into the reception. Hurrying towards the desk, she left him waiting by the potted palm, rattling his keys inside his pocket, while she leaned over the counter to grin at the horse-plaited clerk behind.

'Miss Wenonah Macgregor, please.' Something told her Wenonah would never be a Mrs.

Without looking up, the clerk ran her finger down a two-columned list of handwritten names, then shook her head. 'Macgregor, you say?' she demanded, eyes still fixed upon the register.

'Macgregor,' Agatha repeated. 'Wenonah. Miss.'

'Sorry.' This time she looked up, giving Agatha the plea-
sure of two heavily kohled eyes and a knot of lines around her
mouth to match her hairstyle. A cigarette burned in an ashtray
somewhere around her feet, and she picked it up, taking a
long drag, figuring who was this kid going to tell. 'No one of
that name here.'

'Are you sure?' Over by the palm tree, the taxi driver
harrumphed loudly. Agatha leaned a little lower over the desk.
'But she must be. She sent a card.' She reached into her back
pocket and produced the postcard, matching it up against the
identical one in the plastic stand to her left. 'See,' she told
her, handing it across the desk. 'So she must be here.'

'Once.' The clerk, whose tag identified her as Susan,
tapped the card authoritatively. 'She might have been here
once, maybe even just for coffee and then helped herself to a
card. That's not to say she's here now. Which she isn't.'

Agatha stepped backwards in desperation, then forwards
again under a similar motivation. 'But I've come all the way
from Massachusetts, from Martha's Vineyard, just to see her.
She has to be here. I've got nowhere else to go.'

'Sorry, honey. Not a lot I can do if her name's not on the
list.' She glanced towards the door where the taxi driver was
pacing irritably. 'Can I help you, sir?' she wondered, standing
up to get a better view.

He shook his head and slapped the trunk of the potted
palm, glaring at Agatha. 'Jesus H Christ,' he cursed, to no one

in particular, and, with a last right hook at the palm, he spun around and headed for the door.

Agatha watched him go, wanting to call him back and justify herself, but unable to think of a good defence. She turned to Susan. 'What am I going to do?' she pleaded, tiredness and her mother's genes encouraging her to share the load.

Susan shrugged. She had been doing this job too long to allow herself to get involved. 'If you've really got nowhere else to go, then you can sit down in the lounge for a while, maybe try and get a bit of sleep. There's nobody around this time of night who'll bother you, and when the night porter comes on, I'll tell him to keep an eye.'

Agatha glanced towards the indicated lounge, all orange leather-look armchairs and glass tables.

'I'll even give you a dollar to call your parents if you like, if you promise me you'll do it and not just spend it on a cola from the machine.'

Agatha nodded. 'Thanks,' she murmured. And taking the coin, she trudged across the swirling carpet to the oasis of orange scroll arms. Then she closed her eyes, tucked the petty cash tin under her head, and fell asleep with the dollar still pressed tight inside her hand.

Chapter Fourteen

She was awoken around five by the roar of vacuum cleaners snaking about the reception area and cutting a mean dash between the arms and legs which made up the lounge. Rubbing her eyes, she sat up slowly, her head imprinted with the lock and square handle of the petty cash tin, and as she pressed her skin in an attempt to retrieve her cheeks, she noticed she had dropped the dollar. Standing up, she pushed back the cushion and felt beneath, but when that yielded only a swizzle stick and a book of matches, she turned her attention to the floor. From the far side of the room, a vacuum cleaner droned towards her, warbling as it worked its way back and forth between the furniture, and as Agatha pushed back her chair, determined to find her dollar, a hand on her shoulder caused her to jump.

'This what you're looking for?' it asked, holding up the coin as she turned around to meet the hand.

And at exactly the same moment as Agatha looked up, the woman with the still blaring vacuum cleaner and the domestics uniform looked down.

'Wenonah!'

'Agatha?'

'Oh, Wenonah! They said you weren't here.'

'Well, surprise.' She turned around to kick the button on the cleaner, her face taut and inexpressive.

'Good job I waited. I might have missed you.' Agatha had conveniently forgotten she had had no choice in the matter.

'Good job I was feeling honest and gave you the dollar you'd lost. Plenty of other times I'd just put it in my pocket.'

They grinned at one another, each strangely proud.

Wenonah looked around. 'So you're with my boy then? I knew sending him that postcard was a bad idea.'

Agatha shook her head. 'I didn't expect you to be working here.' She gazed at her overalls, adding, 'I'm by myself.'

Wenonah shrugged, then glanced about. 'Listen, kiddo, I've got a job to do and I can't afford to lose it. You wait while I finish, and then maybe we can go out and get some breakfast. You can tell me what the hell you're doing turning up here at five o'clock in the morning.'

Agatha nodded, and sat back. Wenonah wagged a finger.

'You can't stay here though. They'll skin me if they find out you're waiting for me. And it was hard enough to get this job as it was.'

'But where do I go?'

Wenonah frowned, then reached inside the pocket of her overalls, handing Agatha a key. 'Here, take this. It's in the basement, left out of the lift. I'll come and find you when I'm done.'

'So I'll wait for you downstairs.'

'Yes, but don't touch anything.'

The vacuum cleaner, thus long sucking on a piece of carpet that was now noticeably paler than the rest, turned towards the reception, Wenonah following. Agatha headed for the lift.

The basement was white and glaring, with strip lighting leading in both directions along the hallway, and a floor of marbled grey lino. As she walked her sneakers whined on the rubbery surface, and her eyes, heavy from so little sleep, blinked against the bright lights above. Wenonah's room was at the end of a long line of similar doors, and she hesitated outside, checking the number on the key before letting herself inside. As she entered, a gust of wind hit her from the tiny sliver of window that squinted on to the street just below the level of the pavement, and the room was filled with the noise of clattering feet and snatched conversations. Agatha listened a moment, enjoying the anonymity, then closed the door behind her.

Staring about the room, she was filled with wonder. Every possible surface was covered with reams of newspaper, and those that were not bore the small blue scars of ones that had fallen down. It was like the original beach house, only in miniature. On the floor, several sheets of paper blew listlessly in the draught, some wrapping themselves around a large, unpacked rucksack stranded in the middle of the plastic-matted floor, others just wafting. On the bed a brightly coloured quilt had been pushed to one side, and the pale orange sheets beneath seemed all the sadder for it. Agatha sat down on a corner of the wrinkled bed, and smiled. 'I'm home,' she murmured, picking the clips of the rucksack and peeping inside at the scrunched and dishevelled contents. And then she lay back on the bed, pulled the quilt over her, and waited for Wenonah.

Hours later there was a loud bang on the door and she opened it to find Wenonah, now relieved of her blue checked overall and dressed simply in a knee-length Indian cotton dress.

'Come on,' she instructed, loosening her long grey hair from the bun in which she had restrained it. 'Let's get something to eat.'

They took the stairs up to the car park, skirting around the hotel and out on to the street. Wenonah was silent, fiddling with her now returned room key, every so often glancing round to check that the twittering Agatha was still with her. Just past the hotel, around the corner, she stopped outside a glass-fronted diner, then waved Agatha inside. Ordering a coffee and juice from the cashier as they entered, she gestured for Agatha to pick out something to eat from the plastic lettered board above the counter, and moved towards a booth at the back. Ordering herself a bagel with tuna fish, Agatha joined her there.

'So are you going to tell me what you're doing here?' Wenonah demanded, lighting up a cigarette and flicking the match across the table where it landed just beside the ketchup bottle.

Agatha picked up the match and twisted it between her fingers, watching it spin back and forth like a cheerleader's baton. She took a deep breath, stuck the match in a grimy crack in the table top, and grinned at Wenonah.

'I thought I could come visit with you for a while. I've never been to Philadelphia. I thought I might be able to help you get yourself together again.'

'What makes you think I need to get myself together? And that I'd want you to help me if I did?'

'I know it was you who burnt Herb's things,' she told her, a fact that was totally unrelated but which nevertheless she felt might hold some weight.

Wenonah stared at her. 'So?'

'So . . .' Agatha considered for a moment, 'so I came after you.'

'I can see that.' Wenonah looked up as the waitress approached with her coffee and juice and Agatha's bagel. 'You don't want anything to drink?'

Agatha shook her head.

'And what exactly d'you expect to achieve, just turnin' up like this? Don't you think I've got enough people on my trail without twelve-year-old girls joining the queue?'

'Thirteen. And I'm not on your trail.' Agatha pushed aside her bagel, wishing she had ordered waffles instead. 'I thought that maybe we could be friends.'

Wenonah sighed and lit another cigarette from the butt of the last one. 'Did you?' She pushed the bagel back towards Agatha, then passed her the orange juice too. 'You must be hungry. You'll fade away.'

Agatha ate, keen to appear amenable, and for a few minutes they were silent.

'I like your room,' Agatha announced. Wenonah jumped at the sound of her voice as if she had forgotten all about her. 'Is that what the beach house was like? Primrose always said it had been kind of kooky.'

'It's how I like it. When you're moving about like I do, you need to put a little bit of yourself into a place. Otherwise you might as well be dead, looking at all those white pointless walls.'

Agatha nodded enthusiastically, thinking of her own white pointless walls at home. On the Vineyard.

'Anyway, it doesn't matter what I do, does it, 'cause there's only me has to live with it.' Wenonah looked at Agatha and raised an eyebrow. 'So I please myself.'

Agatha nodded. 'I wouldn't be in your way,' she told her,

seeing this as her cue to speak. 'I'm good at looking after myself and I'm really quiet and tidy when I need to be. You wouldn't know I was there, and it would only be until I found myself a job.'

'Kid, you're thirteen years old.'

'People say I look older. I could pass for sixteen, no problem.'

'Yeah, and I could pass for the King of Spain.'

Agatha concentrated on her half-eaten bagel, playing with a frill of lettuce. 'I promise I'll be good,' Agatha told her. 'Just let me stay a week or so. Please, Wenonah. You're all I've got.'

'And I'm all I've got.' She shook her head. 'No, Agatha. You've got a good home back there on the Vineyard. Go back to it, kid. Grow up a bit. After that we might talk about it. But even then, I don't know that I care for having another person around the whole time. My life's fine the way it is. It doesn't need any fixing.'

Agatha was still staring at the bagel. 'But you have to let me,' she mumbled, her voice thickening. 'I can't go back now.'

'Yes, you can,' Wenonah told her. 'You didn't kill anybody, did you? You haven't set fire to the cat or your father or anything like that? Have you? So, course you can go back. They probably won't even have noticed you'd gone.'

Agatha sank a little lower on her side of the booth, the truth in this last observation surely all the more reason for her to stay. Her chin on the table, she peered at Wenonah through spidered hands, then reached behind her to reveal the petty cash tin. 'I stole this,' she confessed. 'And then I spent it. All of it. I even owe a taxi driver seventeen dollars because I thought I was going to see you last night and you'd be able to lend it to me . . .' She trailed off, staring at Wenonah with 'I told you so' eyes.

Wenonah shrugged dismissively. 'So you stole a few weeks' pocket money, big deal. You can go back.'

'But I don't want to. I want to stay here with you. When you were staying with us things were different. They made more sense.'

Wenonah smiled. False beards, pink hands and the destruction of what little work her father had ever done made 'sense'? She stood up, suddenly, inching crablike out of the booth. 'Wait here.' She disappeared out back.

When she returned she was more relaxed somehow, taking a bite from Agatha's still unfinished bagel and smiling reassuringly. 'Don't worry,' she told her. 'It's all going to be fine.'

And Agatha grinned, leaning forward over her plate, reaching for the elder woman's hand. 'I won't let you down, you know. You won't regret this.'

'I know I won't,' nodded Wenonah.

Chapter Fifteen

When Johnny got the phone call from his mother, he was doubled up on the deck of his boat with a length of masking tape and some Super Glu, attempting a little restoration work. That his mother was on the line was in itself not so unbelievable — although it was the first time she had attempted such communications — but that Agatha was with her, sitting in a diner in Philadelphia eating a tuna bagel and wanting to move in, was.

'Just come and get her,' Wenonah demanded, barking an address at him then hanging up.

'I'm on my way,' he told the lifeless receiver. 'Hold on, I'm on my way.' With the Super Glu tube still in his hand, he grabbed his jacket, slid closed the doors to the boatshed, and headed across the dunes.

He didn't tell Primrose where he was going, didn't even let her know he wouldn't be in that day, just made straight for the main road and hitched a lift to West Tisbury where he knocked on Ben's door and begged him to lend him his cab. With a quick tally of the lost fares and an extra fifty bucks for the mileage it would add, Ben agreed, handing him the keys and muttering something about today being his day off anyway. Johnny nodded, promised him a cheque, and was gone.

It took Johnny Macgregor seven and a half hours to drive to Philadelphia, hurtling up Route 95, desperate to get there before Agatha decided to do something else stupid. He couldn't help but feel it was his fault, her disappearing like this, and he wished he had never mentioned that damned postcard. When he arrived at the Holiday Inn, somewhat overwrought, largely due to what he thought Primrose might say to him if he couldn't bring Agatha back, he pulled into the car park round the back, then sat for a moment or two wondering how to approach this.

But there was no need. Within minutes of turning off the engine and straightening his shirt before getting out, the door to the passenger side swung open, and his mother's face appeared in its place. 'She's coming,' was her only greeting.

He looked out across the expanse of bonnets and windscreens and watched Agatha wander towards them, her steps heavy and despondent. 'Hiya,' he offered, climbing out of his side and walking to meet her. Eyes fixed steadily upon her reluctant feet, she did not answer.

And as he lowered her into the passenger seat, waving to his mother's retreating back as she returned to start her next shift, he heard Agatha murmur something into her chest, then watched as she quietly began to weep.

'What did you say?' he asked, leaning across her to fasten her seatbelt and gently stroking her trembling cheek.

'I said I thought she was my angel,' Agatha repeated, all whim and water.

There was little Johnny could do but shrug.

The drive back passed in silence, Johnny stopping the other side of New York to fill the tank and offering Agatha a burger, for there was a long way to go yet. She shook her head. 'I'm not hungry.'

He bought her one anyway. Dropping it on to her lap, they pulled out of the gas station, and Johnny watched as she wound down her window and threw the burger into the road. 'I'm not hungry,' she repeated.

Johnny thought for a moment, his hands tightening on the wheel but his face still loose. 'What did you mean,' he glanced towards her then turned back to the road, 'when you said about her being your angel?'

'I don't want to talk about it.' Agatha was less enamoured with this idea now she was heading home.

'But you must have meant something.' He leaned across

her to wind up the window, and swerved violently in the attempt. Agatha pushed him away, and wound it up herself instead. Without the roaring wind, the car was calmer, less fraught, and Agatha relaxed a little into her seat. She gazed out the window, thinking for a moment, then sighed.

'All my life,' she told him, 'everyone's been talking about angels. Herb's seen them on cliffs, then somehow ended up going to the cinema with them. Primrose fills buckets full of scraps for hers and lets them sleep on the roof. Even you mention them sometimes.'

'I do?'

'Yes. Lots of times I've heard you call Primrose your angel, when she's done something for you, or just if you feel like it.' She stopped, winding down the window once again and putting her forehead against the crack. 'And I thought Wenonah was mine. I thought I could have something for myself, like you all do. I thought she'd make it better.'

'Then you don't know my mother.'

'But I thought I did. I even thought she and I were similar. But she didn't want me around, not even for a day or so. She called you the minute I wasn't looking.'

Johnny slowed and drifted into the outside lane, ignoring the honking of several cars whose paths he crossed, and sitting at a comfortable 50 mph in the outside lane.

'Anyway, I don't want to talk about it.' Agatha dropped back in her seat and stared resolutely at the flashing monochrome landscape. When he tried to press her further, she

simply flicked on the radio, and when he complained about the
noise, she closed her eyes and pretended to sleep instead.

It was quicker going back, for some reason, and they were at
the ferry in Woods Hole just in time for the last crossing at
11.30. Agatha had maintained her silence all the way down the
coast, and any attempt Johnny made to lighten the mood met
with a deep sigh and another inch of open window. Eventually,
the night air blowing a gale through the car and Johnny shivering violently, he learnt to keep his questions and wonderings to
himself, and by the time they reached the ferry, peace was
made.

'What did you tell them? About coming to get me?'

'Nothing. They don't know.'

'So were they worried? Did they miss me last night?'

'I don't know. I left kind of late, around eleven, and I
think your mother went straight to bed. Herb was still out
wherever it was he'd gone, and I know she just wanted to get
some sleep. You know, could be they never even knew you'd
gone, and I certainly won't tell.'

Agatha nodded. As they drove on to the ferry she stared
at the milling waters beneath the boat and shook her head. 'So
that was my great escape,' she mumbled, fiddling with the
gearstick, then snatching back her hand as Johnny moved to
put it into neutral.

'And now you're back safe and sound, no harm done,' he
reassured.

Agatha rolled her eyes and climbed out of the car to go and stand on deck. 'What do you know about it, Johnny?' She combed her fingers through her flattened hair and pulled up her collar. 'What do any of you know?'

As it turned out, they knew nothing. Or certainly, not about the fact Agatha had been to Philadelphia for two days. As Johnny had suspected, Primrose had gone straight to bed after he had left, assuming Agatha to be in her room in one of her sulks, and when Herb got back, he was equally unobservant. The next morning passed similarly without note, Primrose concluding, simply, that it was going to be one of those days, and hence when Agatha arrived around one in the morning that second night, just after the last of the turkeys, she was met with nothing more than a smile from beneath the sheets and an offer of pie on the table if she felt like supper. With Johnny standing in the doorway behind her, and the tap tap tap of Herb's typewriter telling them where he was, Agatha leant against the doorjamb and wished her life more obvious. But because wishes were proving rather a waste of time, instead she threw a goodnight towards Johnny and headed up the ladder to the attic.

Her room was hot and stifling, and she made straight for the skylight, swinging it open and surprising one of the residents on the roof in the process. Much squawking and gobbling followed, with a couple of heads poked in and out just for good measure, and she sat there, in all that rushing heat, and felt the loss of so much. Downstairs Johnny was talking with Primrose, something about the business and an idea he had for picnic lunches on the boat, and in the laundry room directly below her, she heard her father pause, presumably listening, then start clattering again when he realised it was of no interest.

And while the turkeys might be Primrose's particular project, right now they felt the closest thing to an ally Agatha had in that house, Miss Marple having taken it upon herself some months earlier to move in with Jeannie – it was all the burning that had done it, Agatha was convinced – and she stared up at their heaving bulks, flapping back and forth across the open skylight.

And then she was climbing, jumping up on the chest of drawers it had taken them three days and a hole in the ceiling to get up here, hauling herself through the skylight and on to the roof. A couple of the more nervous members of the company met her arrival with a hasty retreat, flopping back into the dunes complainingly, but when the others just ignored her, offering the more usual response to Agatha's presence, gradually, one by one, they returned. Wings tucked tight against their sides, heads down, they balanced there, every so often surprising both themselves and Agatha as their pastrified weight got the better of gravity and sent them rolling sleepily towards the gutter, a couple of times disappearing altogether, and for the first hour or so she wanted only to watch them. But then, when the wind dropped and the night seemed so still and all those soft feathered bodies looked so inviting, it was hard to go back downstairs to her old single bed. And so she stayed on the roof, one leg hooked around the chimney pot, the other pressed against one of the old guard of turkeys (named Poirot, due to a stripe across his front Primrose liked to think of as a cummerbund). Staring at the glittering sky above and sighing, she leant back against a soft full belly whose identity would only be revealed when the sun rose the next morning, and slowly, regrettably, hopefully, closed her eyes.

After that, she slept on the roof every night, sneaking up once the rest of the house had gone to bed, and returning early next morning as the sky lightened and the birds made their retreat. Even in the depths of winter she was up there, bringing along a bunch of blankets and, when necessary, a tarpaulin to keep off the rain, and as the months and seasons passed, it was the one place she was happy. The remaining sixteen hours of the day, she was still searching.

Chapter Sixteen

Agatha's quest to find something of her own took her far and wide. And when far and wide didn't work, she came home and looked under her bed instead. As a potential angel, Wenonah had been worthless, but as some kind of direction, Agatha was convinced she could be of help. And so she emptied out the boxes of paper and photographs she had so carefully filed away the summer before, and slowly, methodically, began to work her way through the contents. Most of it was cuttings from the *Vineyard Gazette*, some trivial, others more significant, but there were also scraps of paper listing ideas of Wenonah's own, and as she read, her hands black with newsprint, her thoughts in a whirl, Agatha catalogued the information in her mind under the ever broader heading of 'What I Know'.

Agatha put down the last piece of paper and leaned back against the side of her bed, considering the prospect. Miss Marple, back on a custody visit, curled a little tighter on her lap and waited to be told. 'What I know: I know the Battle of Hastings was 1066 and that cranberries are the state's primary agricultural product; I know everything tastes better the day after you make it; and I know that if you want something done properly, you should do it yourself.' A pause. 'I know magpies are lucky if in pairs; flatfish floating on the top of the sea means a storm's coming; boiled seaweed wrapped around a sprain is the best cure; and the only remedy for warts is the breath of a man who has never seen his father.' Silence. 'I know black cats are lucky – that's you, Miss Marple – and . . .' Agatha paused, watching as Miss Marple looked up at the mention of her name, then stretched herself into a curling question mark across the length of Agatha's legs. Staring at her for a moment, Agatha wondered how any of this was about to help her find a purpose in life, but because the only answer was asleep on her knees, and an interrogation in herself, she carried on listing what she had learnt.

From who was where when a car backfired on Main Street in Edgartown, causing a tourist from Florida to drop dead of a heart attack; to what exactly had taken place on the day the owner of the hot dog stall up on Gay Head Cliffs ran his cart over the edge and into the sea below; from why it was that moonshells could only be found at the end of the lunar cycle when the tide is pulled right back; to whoever would have

thought that the Irish moss seaweed Primrose had been using
for years to thicken her pie fillings would catch on commer-
cially as an emulsifier in ice creams.

As the sky darkened above her head and downstairs the
ovens were at last turned off for the day, Agatha remained
there, sorting through her mind, until even Miss Marple grew
weary of listening and disappeared out of the skylight to chase
a few turkeys. And then Agatha stood up, packing all those
papers and lists back beneath her bed, and followed the cat out
on to the roof to see if any of this had made a difference.

But everything was still as it was, no gleaming visions
beneath the lighthouse, no shining wings and haloes, just a dark
sea occasionally flashed by an electric lamp, and a crowd of dirty
old birds trying to get the better of the cat. Agatha sighed, and
took a seat on the crumbling chimney stack. On the beach outside, Primrose waved goodbye to the afternoon's last guests –
Johnny's latest scheme was a liquor licence, which gave rather
more sway to the proceedings – and Agatha listened as the two
of them cleared away the last of the tables and returned to the
kitchen for supper. Herb was in his laundry room, preparing the
last of his data for the Report, due in next week, and the tide
was out, leaving the beach empty and vaguely pathetic, like a
party after everyone has gone home. She sighed, watching as
Miss Marple dropped off the side of the roof and scampered
across the dunes on a short cut back to Jeannie, then herself slid
off the chimney to sit with it flat against her back.

Poirot, always one of the first to arrive, was scratching

irritably at one of the many loose slates, waiting for Primrose to bring supper, and Agatha watched him listlessly, attempting to call him over with a 'cluck' and a 'gobble' she had perfected for the purpose. He ignored her. And so she turned to one of the other turkeys, and then another, holding out her hand and tempting them to approach, but yet again she was ignored.

Only one bird allowed her anywhere near, sitting on the edge of the gutter with its head under its wing, oblivious to its companions flinging themselves every which way as this girl in search of a purpose tried to make them it. As Agatha moved closer it did not even flinch.

'You're nice.' Agatha glared at the others as they gathered on the far side of the roof. 'You're my favourite.'

But Agatha's favourite was in no state to appreciate such declarations, for as she wrapped her arm around its neck in a gesture of affection, her hand met with the wet, warm stickiness of what could only be blood, and jumping back she saw the gutter was filled with the stuff, trickling glueily on to the sand below.

'Oh no,' breathed Agatha, panicking slightly. Stepping backwards, she looked towards the crowd of birds on the other side of the roof. 'Help me,' she demanded, but when none of them moved, she made for the skylight instead.

'Primrose, Primrose, help me,' she squawked, her head and shoulders swinging through the roof and aiming for the square of bright light which was the way down into the hall. In the kitchen, Primrose looked up.

'Did you hear something?' she asked Johnny, not used to getting a summons from her daughter.

Johnny nodded. 'I think it was Agatha.'

Primrose walked into the hall, looking up through the trapdoor into Agatha's room and calling out, tentatively, 'Did you want me?'

'Help me. One of them's hurt and there's blood all over the place.'

Instinctively recognising 'them' to be her birds, Primrose jumped on to the dangling ladder and pulled herself up into the attic. 'Do you mind if I come in?' she checked, glancing up at the batlike Agatha.

'Just hurry, will you,' Agatha begged, holding out her blood-covered arm and waving frantically.

Primrose hurried. Vaulting on to the bed and through the skylight with an agility her thickening pastried waist belied, she took one look at the ailing bird over by the gutter, then began to rant.

'Those bastards! Those bastards are now even aiming at mine.' Pushing Agatha to one side, she put her arms around the bird and lifted it on to her lap. 'I need towels, warm water, the first-aid box from the kitchen, and a set of tweezers which you'll find with my sewing set.' She took a breath. 'And Johnny. Get Johnny.'

Agatha stared for a moment at the picture of her mother cradling the bird, then did as she was told. As she gathered the other things, Johnny found Primrose, and then, between them, they lifted the bird through the skylight and laid it upon Agatha's bed.

'Shot?' asked Johnny.

Primrose nodded. 'How dare they?'

'Do you think we should just . . .?' He mimed a gun with his thumb and forefinger. She flinched.

'Over my dead body. They can't do this, you know. They can't take pot shots at something just because it suits them.'

Agatha appeared at the top of the ladder and handed Primrose the towels and hot water. She gave Johnny the first-aid box and tweezers, then sat down on the floor and watched. All the while talking to the bird in a soft, lilting voice, Primrose turned it on to its side and pressed a towel against it, dipping another in the water and then gesturing for Johnny to hold that there too. Then she took the tweezers and gently plucked out the matted feathers surrounding the wound, passing each one to Agatha, and gently dabbing at the bird's puckering flesh. 'The bullet's still there,' she showed Johnny, as he leaned forward. 'Agatha, get the gin.'

'Gin?'

'Yes, get the gin.' She waved her away, then took a wad of cotton wool from the first-aid box, dowsing it in the reluctantly proffered alcohol and holding it to the bird's beak. Then before either the bird or those watching knew what she was doing, she reached the tweezers into its side and in one move, picked out the bullet.

The turkey screeched in pain, then flapped backwards,

Johnny taking its weight as it hung off the edge of the bed.
Agatha gasped in horror. 'Is it dead?'

'Of course it isn't dead,' Primrose snapped, stroking its
neck. 'But when I find out who did this . . .' She did not finish,
but instead returned to dabbing at the turkey's side, before
wrapping the whole bird up in a mummy of bandages, and
covering it with Agatha's eiderdown. 'When I find out,' she
repeated, looking at Johnny with tears in her eyes. She laid
down beside the bird, her arm resting across its heaving belly,
and shook her head. 'When I find out.'

It was midnight when Herb left the laundry room, wandering around glazed and irritated in the bright of the still
wakeful house. 'Where's your mother?' he asked Agatha, when
he found her perched in front of the television watching
Saturday Night Live. 'Did she go out?'

Agatha shook her head and gestured towards the attic.
'Bird sitting.'

Baffled, Herb wandered into the hall and climbed up the
ladder, to find Primrose lying on the bed in bloodstained
clothes singing lullabies to a sleeping turkey. 'Primrose?' he
checked, hoping his eyes were deceiving him and this was not
her at all.

'Shhhh,' she told him, her finger to her lips. 'She's sleeping.'

Herb pulled himself into the room to stand at the end of
the bed. 'Have you gone completely mad?' He moved to turn
on the main light but stopped when Primrose hissed at him
violently. 'I take it that's one of your turkeys in there, not

Johnny or someone in disguise?' He grinned at the idea of such infidelities.

'I'm glad you find attempted murder amusing. This bird was left for dead by some trigger-happy lunatic, and you think it's funny.'

'I don't think it's funny,' Herb backtracked. 'I'm just rather taken aback by finding you in bed with it.'

'Well, get used to it. Because I'm staying here until she's better.' She shook her head. 'I can't believe anyone would do this.'

'People kill animals all the time, Primrose,' Herb reasoned.

'Not in this house they don't.'

Herb shrugged. 'Well, I'm going to bed then.' He backed away towards the stairs. 'Good night.'

And he climbed down the ladder just as Johnny came through the screen door, carrying armfuls of new bandages and a hammock. 'You too?' Herb asked, but before Johnny could answer Herb had walked into the bedroom and shut the door. 'Completely mad,' he told the four walls. 'Completely and utterly mad.'

That night, just as she had said, Primrose remained with the turkey, soothing its every squawk, promising things would get better. Around dawn they redressed the wound with the new bandages, and as soon as it was light, Johnny set about hanging the hammock, draping it from one side of the room to the other, then between them, lifting the bird inside.

'That should be more comfortable,' he murmured as Primrose fussed with blankets and hot water bottles. She nodded.

'Thank you for helping, Johnny,' she told him, as they made their way back downstairs to the kitchen to turn on the ovens.

'Any time.'

They called the bird Agatha, both because she had been the one to find it and it had slept in her bed, and while the real Agatha was less than flattered by the choice, she was too tired to argue. She had spent the night in front of the television, unsure where else she should go, and by the time Johnny and Primrose appeared she was glazed and confused, wishing only to sleep. And so they changed the sheets and sent her back up with turkey Agatha, and as the two namesakes snored away the day, one beneath the other, the first-named dreamed of a great weight dropping on her, then woke up to find it had.

Thus, with the bird too heavy for the hammock, and Agatha too proud to share a bed, the former got the attic, and Agatha ascended to the roof, dressed in a sun hat and a layer of Factor 10, and with one getting better and the other getting brown, there seemed nothing more to add.

And yet Primrose was not finished. True to her word, she was going to find the culprit, and the very day turkey Agatha was well enough to stand up, and she could trust the others to look after her, she picked up her bag and headed for the cliffs. All day she walked up and down the island's roads, knocking on doors, climbing over fences and challenging farmers, harassing passers-by, until she had collected enough hard stares and 'Given half a chance's' to assure her the world was a wicked place and someone needed to change it.

When she returned home that night, then, Primrose was on a roll. 'Criminals and idiots, the lot of them,' she declared, slamming the door behind her and dropping to the table. 'If you knew how many potential serial killers there are out there, you wouldn't sleep in your beds.' She gritted her teeth angrily and glanced at the record of that day's takings.

Agatha, who had lost such bed-rights anyway, shrugged dismissively and turned up the volume on the television. Primrose turned it down again, then reached for a piece of paper and a pen. 'Something has to be done,' she told the kitchen at large, and Herb, arriving in the doorway at just that moment, twisted his finger against his head, mouthed 'Mad,' and walked out again.

'We have to mount a protest,' Primrose continued, at which point Agatha joined her father. 'We have to save the turkeys.'

And Johnny, all alone there in the kitchen and a sucker for a new idea, nodded enthusiastically, and asked where they should start.

They were up until dawn that night, and for the whole week afterwards, plotting and planning, drilling and banging, and with the attic as their protest headquarters, Herb and Agatha kept to their own places above and below and hoped only for a little peace. With turkey Agatha improving every day, only the bald patch on her side (round and scarred and perfect, as Herb put it, for target practice) kept them focused upon the job in hand, and as summer neared its end and the queues for a table on the deck began to shorten, speculation began to mount as to what they were going to do.

'Wait and see,' Primrose insisted, closing the trapdoor on Herb's upturned face and pulling a curtain across the skylight, attacks of interest coming from both sides. 'You didn't want to know before, why should I tell you now? Let's just say, people will have no choice but to listen to us by the time we're finished.'

But while turkey Agatha sipped at water from one of Primrose's best china cups, Agatha proper was feeling ill at ease. 'You don't think she's going to do something stupid?' she asked Herb, one more humiliation at the hands of her family almost too much to bear. (She was still getting over Herb's recent flirtation with the coast guard, whose son went to Agatha's school.) Hence, when she sneaked into her old bedroom one afternoon while Primrose and Johnny were catering for a private party further down the beach and Herb was on an away-day, it was for no other reason than to protect her reputation.

She had not been in her room for almost a month now, climbing on to the roof at nights via the front deck rather than passing through the attic and being accused of ignoring the cause, and as she opened the trapdoor and moved to flick on the light, she was prepared for an amount of change. But not this much. For everywhere Agatha looked there were shreds of torn sugar paper, curling around chair legs, fluttering across the floor, some even wallpapering the walls, having been wet at some point and allowed to stick. Immediately Agatha thought of Wenonah, and wondered if she had returned, this certainly accounting for the secrecy of the last few weeks, but when she gazed around at the rest of the room, she knew it was even beyond Wenonah. Large cardboard placards leaned like toppled pillars against every vertical surface, some blank, others containing cryptic, newsprint messages Agatha had neither the time nor the inclination to decode, and each bearing somewhere on its flat face the bold, coloured shape of a turkey. Over by her desk, Johnny's toolbox lay open, nails and screws spewed in all directions, and in the midst of this, several lengths of driftwood had been tacked together and fixed to the back of one of the signboards, presumably to aid carrying. On the desk itself, small piles of crayons were arranged like multicoloured mole hills, and behind this the whole length of the whitewashed wall had been graffitied with what she could only presume were practice runs at sketching turkeys. Her drawers stood gaping and empty, and the shelves Johnny had put up to exactly her measurements were stripped of all but the now mandatory shreds of paper, occasionally broken by a couple of stray feathers or a lipstick belonging to Primrose.

Agatha sighed, picking up one of the latter, a small silver

Estée Lauder favourite, which, when opened, she could match directly to the red smeared writing on one of the signboards. Rolling it between her hands, she felt sick, standing here in the midst of all this destructive creativity, and had she had any sympathy for her mother's cause before, now it was gone. Much like her father before her, she saw the one place she felt safe destroyed, only in her case, Agatha considered, it had not been an act of revenge, but one of supreme and ultimately unforgivable indifference.

Leaving everything exactly as she had found it, she climbed back down the ladder and wandered out on to the deck. Walking straight through the lines of tables, she jumped off the steps on to the beach, and made her way to the water's edge. In the distance, the horizon lay soft and sweeping, like velvet on the hem of a dress, and for some time Agatha just stood there staring, wondering what had brought her here. And because she didn't have an answer, she remained there, watching the line at the end of the sea, until long after it had faded into night, long after Primrose was back from her party, long after the turkeys had bounded on to the roof and settled themselves in. Only then, when all the world was still and dark again, except for the odd flurry of hammering from the attic, did Agatha move, but rather than heading for the house, she set off up the beach, feeling her way up the cliff path and knocking on the door to Jeannie's trailer just as the elder woman was climbing into bed.

'Can I come in?' She put her foot inside the door. Jeannie stood back, her old greying nightdress lying across her bony chest like muslin over fruitcake. 'Help yourself,' she offered.

Agatha stepped inside, moving to the bench seat across from Jeannie's bed and sitting down. 'I need to ask a favour.'

'What?' Jeannie climbed back into bed and pulled the covers over her legs to reveal a sleeping Miss Marple curled up beneath. 'Not gone and got yourself into trouble, have you now?'

Agatha shook her head. 'I need you to help me run away. I tried it once already, just by myself, but I made a bit of a mess of it, so I wondered if you could help me this time. To get it right.'

Jeannie grinned. 'I just love running away. Isn't it the best? And of course I'll help you, give you some pointers. I did it myself once, a long time ago, and particularly well, if you'll pardon me bragging. You just tell me what you need to know.'

Agatha relaxed a little. This was going better than she had expected. 'Well, where to go, to start with. And who with. And where to stay when I get there . . .'

'You haven't thought this through very well, have you? I mean, you have to have an idea yourself of where you want to be, else there's really not much point.'

'Oh no, there's every point. You see, I just have to go, to get away from here. It's not where I get that matters so much. It's the going.'

'Yeah, but who's to say when you get to that place, you're not going to want to run away from there too? You might spend your whole life getting places and running away again.'

'I won't. I just can't stay here.'

'You don't have to. But you could at least be a bit more definite. That way, you're running away with a bit of direction.' She lifted her shoulders dismissively. 'I mean, do what you want, but if you're asking for my advice, make your mind up first. It won't get better, but that way you can be sure that what you're running to isn't worse. Make sense?'

Agatha considered for a moment, then nodded. After the disaster of her last escape, she had not exactly relished the prospect of running away again, but standing there staring at the horizon, she had been unable to think of anything better. 'So you're saying I should plan ahead?'

'Sure, draw a few maps, write a few names down. Think of it like a holiday.'

Agatha nodded. 'Mmm. Then, when I've decided exactly where I want to be, I go.'

'Sure, you got it. That's my advice anyway. And I've done it, so I know what I'm talking about.' Climbing out of bed, she reached into the cupboard which ran the length of the trailer and took out a bottle of rum. Taking a swig herself, she handed the bottle to Agatha and grinned as she did likewise. 'You want to stay here tonight?' she offered, moving Miss Marple to one side and gesturing for Agatha to lie down.

'Thanks, but I think I'll go back. I've got plans to be getting on with.' Smiling, she leaned across the bed to stroke Miss Marple, then waved towards Jeannie and let herself out the door. Running back down the cliffs and on to the beach, she felt almost free. Almost.

Chapter Seventeen

It took Agatha two years to decide upon where to run to, years in which she settled and made plans for almost every country within the civilised world, until eventually she plumped for Ireland. Ireland had many advantages, first and foremost being that it was directly on the other side of the Atlantic, so it couldn't be all that complicated to get to, and furthermore, it was significantly better placed than Philadelphia in terms of seven-hour drives which could bring her home again. After many long afternoons spent in the travel section of the Bunch of Grapes Bookstore, her future at last began to take shape, and as she folded together the wreaths of maps and lists which had brought her to this decision, the reasons for leaving seemed somehow easier to bear.

And yet they were not. For, if anything, over the last two years relations had only worsened, Primrose's obsession with her turkeys taking her far and beyond a desire to save them from irritable farmers to a realm none of them watching could even begin to approach. From that cataclysmic day when she and Johnny had stormed the Livestock Show in West Tisbury with their banners and placards, hijacking the podium just as the award for the champion of the wood-chopping contest was being given, and wreaking havoc as only Primrose knew how, she had been beyond redemption. Followed by more than twenty of her loyal roof-tenants, she led turkey Agatha and her bald patch around the winner's circle and told the assembled audience of her need for their support, and when the best they could do was murmur and stare helplessly at the winning woodchopper, she sat down in the middle and declared she could wait. Which she did. For the whole three-day event, she sat in the middle of the winner's circle surrounded by her coven of turkeys, Johnny running back and forth for refreshments, Herb and Agatha scooting home in shame, until at last the organisers lost patience with the thing and arranged to send the prizes by post. If she achieved anything during those three days of protest, she achieved notoriety. Other than that, she was just one more attraction, squeezed between the ferris wheel and the baked goods stall, and a definite 'must see'. But while the protest might have had little effect in as far as saving turkeys was concerned, for Agatha it was one of the few points in her life she could put her finger on and say, 'That was when it changed.' For although the decision to run away had its roots in more than just Primrose's desire to save a shot bird, the day Agatha watched her mother sit down in the midst of the island's great and finest, her pied-pipering birds all around, was the day she gave up for good. She no longer cared when schoolmates made fun of her parents or the eccentric life they led: she simply stopped going to school. What did it matter if most of the customers at the café now came to get a glimpse of the mad bird-woman and ordered pies merely as an after-thought? Agatha was never at home anymore, so why should it bother her? And who gave a hoot if, as a result of Primrose's antics, Herb's job as writer of the Annual Report was cut off in its prime, due to a Town Hall committee that felt lunacy so close to home could hardly make for accurate statistics? Herb would just have to find another excuse for his days out.

Hence, in her newly assumed role as truant and absentee daughter, Agatha had quite some time to fill, and as she climbed on to her bicycle each morning and headed for the cliffs, she had one intention, and one alone: to make money. Running away, according to Jeannie, Agatha's appointed teacher in all things abandoning, did not come cheap.

And so Agatha embarked upon a path of acquisition, one that would stay with her in some form or another for the rest of her life. Whatever she did, she did it for the dimes, and as the dollars slowly began to mount up, she found new purpose in the time-wasting antics of her days.

'Did you hear I became champion of the rings yesterday?'

she announced proudly to Jeannie one afternoon, leaning on
the countertop of her quahog stall and spinning one such ring
nonchalantly around her forefinger. She had recently made an
art form of riding the Flying Horses Carousel in Oak Bluffs,
catching the steel rings which dropped from the chute below
the balcony steps as she swung around, often hanging on to her
mount only by the ankles as she stretched and pirouetted,
always pushing that little bit harder for the single brass ring that
meant a free ride. She had even started taking bets at the
beginning of each ride, approaching innocent tourists and pretending this was all part of the fairground experience, and as
she landed the six or seven she needed to beat the odds, holding out her hand mid-ride for her winnings. The day she caught
her nine rings – that was one on each finger of both hands
except her left thumb, needed for holding on – she had fifty
bucks riding on the challenge, and as she claimed her jackpot,
she was only mildly triumphant.

'Shoulda bet a clean hundred, shouldn't I?' she told the
unfortunate Midwester, who had foolishly assumed the feat
impossible.

And while he counted out his dollars, begrudging the
Wild Turkey T-shirts he now could not afford, she smiled the
poor-me smile that had seduced him into betting on her in the
first place, and disappeared into the crowd to find a taker for
the next round.

'They love me on that carousel now,' she told Jeannie
with a grin. 'They've never had so many people hanging

around, waiting for me to miss a ring, challenging each other to beat me. I told them they should pay a commission, but they're more concerned about me not walking off with the rings.'

'You must be raking it in already, though, no?' Jeannie handed her a cone of chowder.

Agatha shook her head. 'I'm getting there, but it's slow.' And she patted her pocket, revealing nothing.

The Flying Horses shut down in winter, however, and Agatha was forced to find a different source of income, eventually settling for delivering her mother's pies, whistling around the island on her bicycle, shouting through windows, abandoning pie boxes on front lawns, and generally adding an extra dollar or two to each bill to top up her daily rate. When she grew bored with that, her mother soon getting wise to the regular complaints she was getting about the increase in prices, she invested in a crate of reject plastic sharks, bought cheap from the company that provided all the *Jaws* memorabilia the tourists still couldn't get enough of. Borrowing a pot of her mother's red nail varnish, she customised the often finless, misshapen creatures, then sold them on to the gift shops as replicas of Jaws as he was at the end of the film. Pure genius, even if she did say so herself.

'It's the "ironic" version,' she would tell bewildered gift-store owners as they debated whether this was really a product for them. 'This is the '80s. You've got to get with the times.'

And invariably they did.

As did the daytrippers she recruited on to her tours of the celebrity residences, her next great project, which, while short-lived, was perhaps the most satisfying given her love of poking around other people's lives.

'A personal tour of the houses of the rich and famous,' her handwritten leaflet promised, 'by someone who knows.'

And as that someone and her bicycle led the wobbling hordes off the ferry and along the various private drives and beaches she had decided to make her own, it was almost like the old days in the bucket, although happily less wet. Until, that is, the Steamship Authority caught on to her and her very un-Vineyard starspotting, and as each ferry arrived in the dock, warnings would be given over the loudspeaker about the dangers of taking up with such no-gooders as that rather innocent-looking child with the bicycle, and the enterprise ended as swiftly as it had begun.

And then the summer of Agatha's sixteenth birthday, she got lucky. She had recently joined the hordes of kids and students who dived for coins in the harbour as the ferries sidled in and out, waving frantically towards the decks and ducking deep for whatever cent, dime, quarter the passengers saw fit to throw. For her part, Agatha only got her hair wet if it was a dollar she was diving for, often demanding that her challenger show her the money before she wasted her time, and as she tucked yet one more silver coin in the purse she wore around her neck, she congratulated herself on having such a good head for business.

'I'm weeks away from the big $1000,' she had told

Jeannie only that morning. 'Just a few more dives and maybe a bet on the carousel, just for old times' sake, and I'm out of here.'

Jeannie nodded, wondering what advice she might delay her with this time. 'How's Herb?' she asked, never having met a daughter yet who couldn't be weakened by a reference to her father.

'Bumming about as usual,' Agatha told her. 'Getting fat on all that carbohydrate Primrose pumps into him.'

Jeannie nodded. She had noticed he wasn't looking his usual healthy self recently. She said so.

'There's only the turkeys healthy in that house, these days,' Agatha muttered, Primrose seeming to find a new bird to nurse almost every week now. 'Do you know how many of the things there are on the roof most nights now? Almost forty. One day the whole lot are just going to come crashing through – bang – killing whichever poor soul was careless enough to sleep in their own bed that night.' Agatha frowned, having poked her head into the attic only that morning to find it starched and hospitalised and full of squawking birds called Agatha.

'She's doing a lot of good, though.' Jeannie was one of Primrose's few supporters, albeit a silent one. 'Someone has to stick up for the little creatures.'

'And someone has to live there.' She pulled a face, then added, triumphantly, 'But not for long.'

'And you're still stuck on Ireland?'

'Yup.'

'But isn't your father from there? Won't it be the first place they look for you?'

'They won't look, Jeannie. They've been here twenty years, and barely moved a muscle. They're not about to start hopping off continents, no matter how much they might say they cared.'

'You really believe they wouldn't miss you, don't you?' Jeannie asked, unusually softly.

Agatha shrugged. 'I just don't think they'd miss me enough to follow, that's all.'

And because Jeannie didn't think so either, having spent the last sixteen years looking down upon a child bobbing about in a bucket, building towers with clamshells, sleeping on the roof, she could only nod. 'Well, I hope you find what you're looking for.' She leaned across the counter and kissed her sunburnt cheek. 'And I hope you send me a postcard when you do.'

Agatha grinned and wiped away the gesture with the back of her hand. 'I'll be fine.' And with that she was away, skipping on to her bicycle and hurtling off along the state road to meet the next ferry in either Oak Bluffs or Vineyard Haven, wherever her timetable told her she could get to first. 'Course I'll find what I'm looking for,' she told the world as she pedalled past it, her words fluttering in the breeze that raced by on either side. She just didn't expect it would be quite so soon.

Agatha was in the sea when he arrived, her green Speedo

costume almost invisible in the murky waters of the dock, and as she blinked up at the bilberry blue sky her only concern was whether the passengers on the 10.24 into Oak Bluffs were in a spending mood. Treading water as her fellow swimmers dived for the pennies, she looked about for someone who was worth a dollar or two, every so often dipping her head just below the surface to show she was game. A woman in pedal-pushers waved a quarter at her on the far side of the deck, but Agatha ignored her, still searching, and just as she began lazily back-stroking her way towards the dock, figuring they were not worth the trouble and she'd find richer pickings in Vineyard Haven, her eyes caught on a figure hanging low over the railings, and she stopped short.

It was his silver sneakers she noticed first, peeking out beneath the bottom rail and glittering like cat's eyes caught in a beam. Immediately remembering Michael – a memory never far from her thoughts since reading Herb's pages – she quickly followed the trail of laces, up the bare legs to the head, which, gazing back down on her with half a smile, she gratefully did not recognise. Agatha shook the saltwater from her spiking hair and stared harder. Wondering if she had ever seen a face quite so full of light, and not imagining for a moment it was just the midday sun on his untanned skin, she blinked once or twice, then returned her attention to the sneakers. At least she knew where she was with these.

He spoke to her, leaning a little lower still over the railings and cupping his hands. 'What's your name?'

'Agatha.' Her arms splashed circles at her sides as she struggled to stay afloat beneath the weight of the moment.

'You want me to throw you something, Agatha?' he asked, grinning teasingly.

Agatha nodded, never one to miss an opportunity.

'You ready?' He felt in his pocket, then held up a dollar. That was more like it. 'Here.' He flicked it up in the air and let it drop, spinning and twinkling as it cut the surface to Agatha's left, and with a kick of her feet she went after it, catching it about ten feet down and rising back to the surface a dollar richer.

But when she opened her eyes he was gone. And the space where he had been was now filled with the pedal-pusher woman, still holding out her quarter. Agatha looked around frantically, searching the sliver of light beneath the bottom rail for just a glimpse of silver, but finding in its place flip-flops and tennis shoes like always.

'Typical.' She dropped her chin beneath the surface and fish-mouthed the salty water. Sliding the dollar into her purse, she rolled on to her back and drifted back towards the side of the harbour, leaving the quarter for those foolish enough to bother, and resolving never again to look twice at a man with spangled shoes.

Climbing up the ladder, Agatha slid the flats of her hands over her wet hair, then moved to pick up her pile of clothes. Pulling on her shorts, she watched as the cars began to ease on to the ramp, the ferry clanking loudly as it rocked in the tide, unaware of the figure wandering towards her along the edge of the dock, sidestepping mooring ropes and the occasional dead crab. Only when he was at her side, hand held out in welcome, did she notice him, but once her hand was in his and those sneakers were glittering at her again, she couldn't have imagined anything less.

'Agatha, you say?'

She nodded.

'I'm Jamie.'

She nodded again.

'So did you find it, my dollar?'

She grinned, patting her purse. 'Always.'

'Then treats are on you.' And with a wave to his departing parents and a promise he would join them later, they wandered side by side off the ferry landing and on to the street, Agatha still carrying half her clothes, he pretending not to notice.

Chapter Eighteen

Treats, that first afternoon, started off as nothing more exciting than a couple of mango ice-creams on the harbour, but even as Agatha licked the last of hers off her wrist and fingers, it was clear this was just a taste of things to come. For already Jamie was suggesting she show him the island, 'the grand tour', as he called it, and although she was quick to insist she did not do that sort of thing any more, that he wanted to spend time with her was clear.

Agatha was curious. Never having been in the position of turning down attentions – largely because they had never really been offered – she struggled to do much except nod and wonder what was wrong with him. Clearly this was not the response he usually got.

'Why are you looking at me like that? Have I got something . . .' He began patting at his face for smears of ice-cream. Agatha shook her head. 'Then what is it? What're you pulling that face for?'

'I'm not. This is always my face.' Now patting her face too, as if to prove that, yes, this was the way it was, Agatha shrugged apologetically and stared at the tipping waves as they lifted and fell against the harbour wall. 'If you knew me better, then you'd know that.'

'Then tell me something about you.'

'Tell me about you first,' Agatha asked, guessing that her 'Nothing to tell' stock answer would do little to solicit confessions in him.

'All right. What do you want to know?'

'Whatever you want to tell me.'

'Well, I'm from Sheffield, which is in the north of England . . .'

'Sheffield Steel,' confirmed Agatha, the writing on her mother's knives suddenly making sense.

'Steel exactly. My dad's a property developer, and he's setting up a shopping centre kind of place in Sheffield, you know, like a mall, so we've all come away to do a bit of a recce to see what you lot do well, and what we don't like so much. But my mum got bored and told him she needed a proper holiday, not just driving around car parks, so we came here.'

'My mother's English,' Agatha revealed.

'Bet she's not from Sheffield.'

'No.'

'I can always tell.'

'And was it in Sheffield that you bought those?' Agatha was back to the sneakers again.

'My mum got them for me. D'you like them?'

'They're okay.' She was still staring at them. 'Where are you staying?'

'Charlotte Hotel. Do you know it?'

'Charlotte Inn,' Agatha corrected. 'Very smart.' She did not tell him that her most memorable experience of the place was when they threw her out of the lobby after she had led a troupe of cyclists through the English gardens because she had a hunch Neil Diamond was staying there.

'So what about this tour? Why not show me around this place? We're here for two weeks so you and I might as well get to know each other.'

Where the 'might as well' came into the equation, Agatha was unsure, but given that she had nothing better to do and there wouldn't be another ferry for at least forty minutes, she nodded. 'So where d'you want to start?'

'You tell me.'

'Then let's start with the Flying Horses.'

That first week Agatha took him everywhere, rediscovering the island for herself as well as him, and at times almost sorry she had decided to go. She showed him the places she had sailed to in her bucket, all those years ago, and the wooden stake she had been moored to still stuck with threads of purple wool; she showed him her father's lighthouse, chasing him around it two or three times just to give him the full picture; she introduced him to the rebel gang of wild turkeys who had rejected Primrose's attentions and set up camp just inside the gates of the Wampanoag territory; she even snuck him into her old bedroom one day when no one was looking just to give him an idea of what she had to live with. In seven short days she shared with him both past and present, and when, on the eighth, it occurred to her that she was in love, she was ready to offer up the future too.

It was Tuesday. Nine days besotted and still refusing to meet his parents – she had two of her own too many, what would she want with his? – Agatha was in high spirits after beating her own record with the rings, and even Jamie was ten dollars down for doubting it.

'I'll take an I.O.U,' she grinned, handing him a pen and one of the coveted rings.

Jamie took both ring and pen and studied them carefully. 'Where now?' he asked as he watched her return the remaining nine rings to the kiosk. 'Now I'm broke it'll have to be very cheap.'

Agatha looked about for inspiration. 'Ice-cream?'

He shook his head. 'No money.' He handed her a scrap of paper on which he had scribbled his I.O.U.

Agatha considered. 'We could do the nature reserve, that

costs nothing.' She took the piece of paper and stuffed it inside
the pocket of her shorts. Snapping the strap of her Speedo –
she had decided it was her lucky costume and hence kept it on
all week – she took his hand and pulled him towards Circuit
Avenue, pointing out the Trinity Park Tabernacle above the
trees, but agreeing when he urged that they leave it for another
day.

'I just want us to spend some time alone together,' Jamie
urged, pressing the brass carousel ring into her back. 'Just you
and me.'

And because 'just you and me's were new to Agatha, she
happily led the way.

She took him to Sengekontacket pond, just south of Oak
Bluffs, naming birds and grasses as they walked, occasionally
stopping to give him a better look, but when at last he told her
he didn't care about such things, and could do with resting for
a while, she nodded and stopped where she was.

Pulling at her Speedo, the brass ring still cutting circles in
her back, he then laid her down in the not-so-interesting beach
grass and gently stroked her hair while she struggled for something non-botanical to say but could only manage an 'Oh'.
And then his fingers were inside the strap of her costume,
yanking it from her shoulder, kissing her neck, while Agatha
concentrated upon breathing in and out and wondered if that
was an osprey she'd just seen fly overhead. And then his hand
was lower, feeling for her breast, missing it, coming back for a

second attempt, Agatha still breathing, still watching for that osprey, wishing he would stop but unsure what she would be preventing. And then he was on top of her, his Sheffield Steel hands on her waist, his rising shoulders now blocking that square of reassuringly blue sky, and as Agatha strained to catch one last glimpse of her bird, she at last figured that the osprey was in fact a particularly large gull, and dropped backwards on to the sand.

Sharing her relief, although oblivious to the osprey question, Jamie fell on top of her once more, still now, although, for him too, breathing was difficult. Agatha watched his forehead twitch a little, then go smooth, and as he rolled over to lie beside her, she noticed for the first time how freckly he was.

'You must burn really easily,' she observed, touching his nose tentatively.

He shrugged, eyes closed.

She waited for him to sit up again, say something, but he just lay there, his chest heaving, the sun clashing with his fair skin and making his features somehow more brittle, less kind. Easing herself on to her elbows, Agatha looked down at her dishevelled body, her Speedo stretched around the top of her thighs, pinching her flesh tight and puckered like those metal tags her mother twisted around her freezer bags. And suddenly she saw not the boy she had decided only hours before was her future, but instead one of her mother's turkeys, fat and contented, and for all the world looking like he had just eaten a good breakfast. Reaching to retrieve her costume, pulling it high, she began to sob, loud and rasping, and as her body wracked with nausea, she bent forward across her unknown knees and gagged into the sand.

It had all happened too fast for Agatha, nought to sex in half a day, and as she pulled her shorts over her feet, her fingers battling ten buttons where in fact there was just one, her only thought was to get away.

'I have to go,' she mumbled, stepping backwards, and as Jamie glanced up, grabbing for her retreating ankles and wondering what was wrong, she turned and ran as fast as she could back towards the road.

Chapter Nineteen

Angels and turkeys, they would get her every time. As she ran, gasping and heaving, back towards the Flying Horses where she had left her bicycle, Agatha cursed all things winged and wanting, and promised herself never again.

Kicking out on to the up-island road, she leaned hard upon the handlebars, and for the first time in a lifetime of looking, saw where she needed to go. Pedalling harder, she pitched herself at the last hill before the beckoning lighthouse and as she rounded the corner, stumbling off the bicycle to fall into the creamy tangles of Queen Anne's Lace that frilled the cliffs, her throat was raw and her nose streamed. Busy serving her early evening chowders, Jeannie did not notice as Agatha stumbled towards the path then tripped her way down it, landing on the beach with a thud and stepping over the few remaining sunbathers scattered on the sand like casually dropped peach stones.

Wheeling her bicycle, she was running again, the wheels skidding in all directions, the pedals cracking against her legs, and when she neared the house she saw her mother on the deck, putting away the last of the tables, and Johnny just behind her. And then Agatha was at the top of the steps, gasping for breath, staring at her mother with this man she had known too long, and hating that for them today was just a Tuesday, because for her it was the end of the world.

At the sound of her wheezing, Primrose turned around. 'Oh hello. Did you have a good day?'

Agatha rushed towards the screen door, unreplying, but Johnny blocked her way.

'Are you okay, Agatha?'

She nodded shakily. 'Excuse me.'

Johnny remained where he was. 'Do you want to talk about it?'

Agatha watched as her mother picked up the last of her scallop-shell ashtrays and stacked them on a tray, balancing it against her aproned front and all the while glancing towards the roof from where the odd squawk and scuttle reminded each of them that they were not alone.

'I'd better get their supper,' Primrose declared, rubbing at the ribbon of skin on the back of her neck that divided collar and pigtails.

Agatha nodded, sidestepping Johnny and seeing this as her moment to escape.

Johnny caught her arm. 'You sure you're okay?'

'Of course.'

And as she barged through the clattering screen door, all fists and shaky breathing, Primrose muttered something about 'probably just hungry' and followed her inside to fetch a pie.

Agatha didn't tell anyone she was leaving, not even Jeannie, simply waited until it was dark, when she could sneak out the back door with her savings and a bag of clothes, then walked back along the beach to the cliff path, watching the tide crash against the clay and the lighthouse up above flash warnings to all who came too close. Remembering for a moment those maps and lists beneath her bed, she wondered if she should go back for them, but because none of this now seemed planned or wished for, she decided there was no point. All she wanted now was to go. Anywhere. Escape. And as she crept up the path, past the brightly lit windows of Jeannie's trailer, she heard squawking like gunfire on the beach behind her and was glad.

Until she got there, she did not know where she was going, but when she reached Squibnocket and Johnny's boathouse it somehow made sense. Staring at the double doors and padlock, she had no qualms in pulling out one of the mooring rods from the marsh where Johnny had once secured his dinghy and using it to lever open the lock, smash the hinges, feel her way inside. Suddenly what she was doing went beyond trespassing or breaking and entering and became her right, her salvation, and as she stared at her reflection in the glass-bottomed boat, the moon glinting off the water and lighting up her face, she caught a glimpse of something more.

And suddenly all her angels were there, in that damp dank boatshed, draped across the rafters, slithering on the glass deck, and Agatha understood what it was the others had missed. What it was they had failed to teach her. As she climbed into the boat, feeling her way towards the bow, then leaning over it to open up the slip doors, her panic was gone, replaced by an overwhelming sense of calm, and when the silence of the water hit her and the only sound was the krik-krak of the marsh frogs and the gentle whoosh of the boat cutting across the pond, she seemed to have wings of her own.

Only two people saw Agatha gently ease Johnny Macgregor's pride and joy out into the bay, allowing the boat to drift until it hit slightly deeper waters, and then thrusting it into life with a quick turn of the engine and a hand to the throttle. Standing over on the bank by the summer bike ferry stand, they were at the time more interested in the possibility of getting a lift across to the Lobsterville Road, waving frantically the minute they noticed her, but in days to come, briefly famous as the last people to see Agatha, they would claim they had known something was odd about it. It was the way she looked back as she swung the boat out towards the Sound, they would say, her hand to her eyes, almost dreamlike, before crouching down and accelerating across the waves and towards the disappearing horizon. It was the way she had seemed almost to fly.

Chapter Twenty

Agatha had been gone over an hour when the storm broke, lifting across the Atlantic like an avenging ghost, and within
minutes the island was wrapped in a cloud of belting black
rain. Back at the house, shutters were slammed closed, pastry
buckets hauled into the dry, and some thirty or forty turkeys
bundled through the skylight into the attic and urged to keep
the noise down. Agatha was missed only as an extra pair of
hands, and even then, Johnny having stayed on to catch up
with paperwork, they could manage perfectly well without
her, and hence it wasn't until much later that they thought to
wonder where she had gone. Later still, they thought they'd
better check with Jeannie, her trailer usually the first place
Agatha would run to, but when Jeannie claimed she had not

seen her since the previous morning, even Primrose found a gap in her routine to worry that something was wrong. And then Johnny went home to his boatshed to get a change of clothes and found it gaping open and the boat gone, and as the island's shore began to gather the usual detritus that followed a storm, he put two and two together and realised that so had Agatha.

'She's gone,' observed Primrose, her voice flat and empty as she moved outside to watch the gaping sea. 'Agatha's gone.'

'We'll find her though,' urged Johnny, determination almost as good as a promise. 'Don't worry.'

'But what if we don't?' asked Herb, joining Primrose at the railing and swaying a little in the cool pink of morning.

'We will,' repeated Johnny. 'We'll find her.'

Above their heads gulls circled, screeching their good mornings as the last of the turkeys squeezed themselves through the skylight and made for the battered dunes.

'We have to,' muttered Herb.

And as all three nodded soberly, a fisherman off Nantucket found a piece of glass deck and a rudder and radioed the police.

After that night Johnny never went back to his boatshed, instead returning to his childhood bed on the sofa, while Primrose replaced Agatha on the roof and Herb remained exactly where he was. For without Agatha there, it all seemed so much less sure, and believing her now gone for good, and not just for an hour in the bucket or an afternoon beyond the cliffs, what they were living for began to lose its point. Within months of Agatha's disappearance, Primrose had sold the Wild Turkey Café to a Japanese businessman who wanted to use the name and the Est. 1970 to front a chain of similar pie houses in the Far East, and within weeks of that she had bought an old van she could convert into an ambulance, hand-painting a red cross on both sides, and officially set up the house as a turkey sanctuary. As Johnny lamented the loss of profit and Herb lamented the loss of a daughter, Primrose concentrated on the diminutions she knew best, and slowly, gradually, misplaced what was left of her turkey-gobbled mind.

And so the house on the beach battled on, each year its walls bowing that little bit wider, each year its eaves dropping that fraction nearer the sea. While Primrose chased across the fields and beaches of up-island, hanging banners from trees and signboards from willing – or not so – arms, Johnny played chief cook and bottlewasher as they nursed their most protested guests. And Herb? Herb grew thin on leftovers and thinner on patience, wasting most of his days wandering in circles around the lighthouse as he lamented the loss of the only thing he could ever have called his own and wondered if he could survive without it. Gradually, his skin turned from tan to grey, his face from full to haggard, and as his rings around the lighthouse became ever fewer, only Jeannie saw the depth of his decline.

'Are you all right?' she asked one afternoon, as he stood staring up at the lamp, wavering from one foot to the other.

'I brought her here the day she was born,' he told Jeannie, still staring.

'Do you want to sit down?' Jeannie wondered. That she had not stopped Agatha more effectively was the greatest regret of her life.

'She started life here, and she ended it here,' he mused. 'She'd have seen this light from where she went down, you know.'

'I know.'

'If we'd been watching, we might have seen her too.'

'You'd never have seen her. None of us would. There was nothing we could do.'

'If we'd known, if we'd been watching, then we could have done something.'

Jeannie shrugged. 'Do you want to sit down?' she asked again, backing towards her trailer.

Herb shook his head, looking once again at the lamp. 'I want Agatha.' And the thin man with the ever-shortening strides began once again to wail.

Chapter Twenty-One

When the storm hit the boat, Agatha had simply hung on tight, the flashes of lightning and rumbling thunder seeming the perfect send-off, and when she hit the rocks just off Tuckernuck Island and the deck began to splinter and spill rushing water, she never once let go her grip. As the waves crashed against her braced legs, the boat tipping and swilling and every minute that little bit lower in the ocean, Agatha looked up at the spinning sturgeon moon above her head and checked her pocket for her savings. And then with a calmness that some might put down to shock, but was in fact a habit with a child used to such turmoil, she put her bag of clothes into the now flooding hold, zipped up her jacket and threw herself overboard. Half swimming, half drifting, she was dragged this way and that under a screeching sky, eyes closed and accepting, until just when she was about to give up and go under, a light up ahead flashed upon her face, and she looked up to see the lighthouse. Vaguely disappointed to be home again so soon, she nevertheless was not fighting as the waves threw her on to the beach and left her there, and while she lay feeling the sand beneath her back and her body shuddering in relief, she felt only cold.

She must have slept or something, for when she opened her eyes the sky was palest grey and on the horizon cracked eggs spread their yellow across the now still sea. Hauling herself to her feet, she turned around to find that the cliffs she had assumed were behind her had moved at some point in the night, and in place of the once familiar lighthouse she saw a rubblestone copy, gleaming new and bright and nothing like what she was looking for. For a moment, Agatha could do little more than stand and stare, the pieces of the place not quite fitting together, and when she began the walk up the beach she had no idea where she was heading.

She must have walked for over an hour, her clothes dripping wet and stuck to her body, putting one foot in front of another because she could not think of anything better to do, and by the time she reached the small wooden hut she had quite given up on the prospect of civilisation. But a woman in safari pants and a Tilley hat had nothing of the same nonchalance, and when she saw the shivering child with the teaspoon eyes she couldn't get her inside fast enough.

'What happened to you? Have you had an accident? How did you end up like this?'

Agatha shrugged. 'Swimming,' she offered, not wanting to give away too much.

'You went swimming? In this weather? Fully dressed?'

Agatha nodded. 'I lost my other clothes, though.'

The woman, Lizzie, shook her head. 'Take them off. Just take them off and I'll give you something of mine. Here,' she handed her a sweater and pair of rainproof trousers. 'These'll do for now, then you can have your own things back when they dry.'

Agatha did as she was told, glancing around the wooden hut at the maps and photographs and hooks hung with binoculars. 'Where am I?'

Lizzie shook her head. 'My, you are in a state, aren't you?'

Agatha shrugged.

'You're on Great Point, my dear, Nantucket. Where on earth did you think you were?'

That Agatha had only made it as far as Nantucket, just across the Sound and a dirty word on the Vineyard, was initially something of a disappointment, given she had been heading for Ireland, but when she considered the alternatives – all the starker in the bright light of day – she decided to be grateful for small mercies and stuck around. After some insistence and a great deal of nagging from Lizzie, she eventually overcame

her shrugging and avoidance of all questions, to create a whole
life history for herself based around the central idea of being an
orphan, and bringing in many a tragedy and torment to prevent the possibility of any return. Only the swimming idea
ever caused any confusion, the much publicised discovery of a
glass-bottomed boat just off the coast suggesting something of
a connection, but when Agatha denied all knowledge of the
thing and claimed she had been on the island for weeks,
nobody took it further.

And hence, newly recreated and calling herself Jane –
after Miss Marple, the only one she imagined she might miss –
Agatha fitted right into her new life on Nantucket, largely
because it was not that different from the one she had had just
across the Sound. Offering herself as a volunteer ranger on the
wildlife sanctuary that was Great Point, in time she was made
a member of staff, complete with cabin and two meals a day,
and basking in her newfound freedom she went from strength
to strength. When she was asked to make the lighthouse part
of her patrol area, she was more than happy to oblige, often
spending whole days clearing driftwood and polishing the solar
panels that had been added when a storm blew the old tower
down a couple of years before and this newer one had been
built. In a way, it was here she felt most at home, gazing out
across the crashing sea and imagining those she had so easily
left behind, and on a clear night she believed she could even see
the house, crouched just below the flashing Gay Head light and
appearing smaller each time. But not once did she think of

going back; not even of sending a postcard: like Herb and Primrose before her, it was a matter of pride.

And yet she did go back once, late one night when the sky was still and black and the sea was flat, something in the air telling her she should visit, and when she watched her mother and Johnny struggling with that bin bag, she knew almost immediately that they were up to more than a little illegal dumping. As they tipped it over the edge of Johnny Macgregor's replacement dinghy, she watched it splash, then float, then sink, the weight of the flour bags and typewriter dragging it from her sight long before she was ready to let it go.

Agatha never quite forgave herself for not being there when Herb died, although such was her inheritance she learned to live with it, and in time she could tell herself it was all for the best. Occasionally, over the years, when her job as Chief Ranger would allow it, she took a boat out and put up a flare for him, this being the best way she could think of to acknowledge a life lived so much in the firing line. And invariably, whenever Primrose saw them, stopping what she was doing to stare at the horizon, she would turn to Johnny, or turkey Agatha, or turkey Agatha's many acquaintances, and insist it was a sign.

'Agatha's out there,' she would tell whoever still cared to listen. 'I tell you, she's watching us.'

And while her audience considered it was perhaps time she revisited that clinic, Primrose nodded knowingly and watched the smoke on the horizon waft and then disappear. Only Herb could have added any weight to her theory, angels and faces in the mist always his big thing, but because any substance he had was now on the bottom of the sea, Primrose struggled on alone.

'Laugh all you like,' she told them, still staring at the beach and unnoticing of Johnny as he picked up the telephone book and looked under C. 'She's out there, whatever you lot might like to think. My Agatha. My angel. She's there.'